MURDER THROUGH THE MIRROR

A POSIE PARKER MYSTERY #14

L. B. HATHAWAY

WHITEHAVEN

WHITEHAVEN MAN PRESS

First published in 2023 by Whitehaven Man Press

(http://www.lbhathaway.com, email: permissions@lbhathaway.com)

ISBN (e-book:) 978-1-913531-28-7
ISBN (paperback:) 978-1-913531-29-4

Also by L.B. Hathaway

The Posie Parker Mystery Series

1. *Murder Offstage*

2. *The Tomb of the Honey Bee*

3. *Murder at Maypole Manor*

4. *The Vanishing of Dr Winter*

5. *Murder of a Movie Star*

(The stand-alone novella, *A Christmas Case*)

6. *Murder in Venice*

7. *The Saltwater Murder*

8. *Murder on the White Cliffs*

9. *Marriage is Murder?*

10. *Murder in the London Lights*

11. *Murder in Tuscany*

12. *Murder in a Chelsea Garden*

13. *Murder and the Mermaid*

14. *Murder through the Mirror*

15. *Murder on the Night Train to Paris*

For the forgotten places.
And the places whose importance ebbs and flows.

a tiny silent village a mile outside the town. This 'special place' felt like the back of beyond.

The middle-aged driver of the motor-taxi from Canterbury station looked at her in a bemused way when he dropped her off on the icy pavement.

She was on a bridge with white painted railings; a tinkle of water sounding clearly below.

A carved wooden sign declared the location was 'HARBLEDOWN', and wisps of grey mist choked the air thickly, suffocatingly. It was as if one of the boss's smoke machines at work had malfunctioned in some way.

The taxi-driver sat with his engine still running.

'It'll be getting dark soon, love,' he said calmly from his rolled-down window. 'You sure you've got the right spot?'

She steadied herself on her heels and pulled out the note. She read aloud: 'The Black Prince's Well, Harbledown?'

The taxi-driver tutted: 'The Well? Did you think it was a pub, Miss? Only, there ain't a pub in Harbledown by that name. The only one here is the Coach and Horses.'

He waved a thick finger in the direction his motor-car was facing, back towards the city. 'They do a good pint and pie; famous for it. Maybe you've got your wires crossed? The wrong name?'

'No, sir.'

She shook her head determinedly. The man she was meeting would never have got his wires crossed. Precision defined him, it had to; accuracy ran through him like his life-blood.

'The instructions I have are correct, sir.'

'Very well then, love.' The taxi-driver pointed somewhere behind her, near the wooden village sign.

'If it's truly the Black Prince's Well you're after, you need to take a sharp left just after this bridge, and walk a minute or so through the undergrowth. The Well is on the left-hand side, you'll see it, no problem. It's stony grey, like a gravestone. It's probably neglected now, overgrown:

I reckon this village lost a lot of their boys in the Great War, and I expect they've been mourning their recent dead rather than worrying about things which happened here hundreds of years ago. I heard the villagers have been saving up for a big Great War memorial for their lads, and it will go up soon.'

The taxi-driver was reluctant to leave.

'I ain't been out here to the Black Prince's Well since I was a boy, but I daresay it's still the same. Tis the stuff of local legend: a place for ghosts, hauntings, fairies. And magic. It's known as a place giving magic cures for ailments and illnesses. A load of stuff and nonsense, of course! At the end of the day, it's a place for desperate people wanting answers to their problems.'

Well, don't we all want that? the girl thought to herself, but she didn't say it aloud, at the risk of seeming disrespectful.

Instead, she waved cheerily and started to walk away.

She was used to men being protective of her.

It was her face. It had been her fortune to be born with a beautiful face; a China-doll's face and blue, blue eyes.

Her face often got her noticed, but it had recently changed her destiny.

A destiny which meant that soon, hopefully, she'd get well away from these terrible cold damp English winters for ever. She'd be away from the grey grubby hopelessness of King's Cross and she'd escape to the heady fame and riches of America.

New York, to be precise.

She'd been offered it. For certain, by a man whom fate had thrown her way.

A kind young American man with a big brain and a big, bulky frame and even bigger dreams. And he'd promised her a future as his partner which combined both love and work.

Fantastic, glittering work; the likes of which the world had not yet seen.

So what if she didn't love him? Not yet, anyhow. She could learn to, couldn't she? And she'd simply pretend until then. Gracious, she'd even agree to go on dates in strange places to keep up the pretence!

Because *he* was her escape.

New York.

She kept a souvenir postcard of the famous skyscrapers tacked onto her dressing-table mirror at the theatre.

It was all going to be okay. Perhaps - at last - she'd even get rid of the awful cockney accent which was the legacy of her childhood, that she'd spent the last few years desperately trying to lose.

She'd stamp all over it with bright new American tones, giving herself a new voice, which was just right for the stage.

There were a few technicalities to sort out before she left England with him.

Easy things; paperwork, really. But not just for herself, because in her life she'd never had the luxury of doing things alone.

But she smiled now as she thought of the far-away city of skyscrapers as she walked along near a hedge, careful of the patches of sheet ice.

Suddenly she heard a horrible screech of brakes further off, up on the road. Then there was a blast of an indignant horn, and what sounded like a sharp yell of pain.

The girl stopped, all senses alert to trouble. A far-off, urgent ringing of a bell was jangling in warning. A police motor-car, perhaps?

But it faded.

And then everything was quiet. Perhaps it had been nothing? An accident averted? A near miss?

The girl was totally alone.

The mist, the twilight, the crunch of the gravel and dirt and the ice underfoot lent the place an unearthly feel. Her breath came in bursts on the cold still air.

It was freezing.

She thought cheerily of hot drinks, of coffee, but laced through with something stronger.

A good Irish coffee with whisky, and heaps of sugar, and cream, all mixed in. Americans drank that, didn't they?

Perhaps they'd order one each up at the pub the old taxi-driver had been wittering on about just now?

They'd drink the Irish coffees together, next to a good open roaring fire, when her date would explain all of *this* to her...

Why they had had to meet *here*. In this odd place. Why it was special to him.

She came upon it suddenly, quickly. The half-darkness couldn't hide it, and the fronds of frozen ferns, and the boughs of yew and oak and ash and alder couldn't conceal it, much though they tried.

It was a rounded arch of grey, soft, chalky stone, set back in a wall, with three feathers carved above it all, and below, a rounded area full of water, like a basin.

A burbling, gurgling noise could be heard.

She stepped right up to it. Peered down.

This must be it, she thought.

The Black Prince's Well.

It was more like a spring-head, the source of a small river. And the water itself was quite shallow, only a foot deep, maybe; the stones visible through the crystal-clear water, like caramel-coloured pebbles on the beach. Ice was forming around the edges.

But the taxi-driver had been wrong about one thing.

The place was not forgotten, or deserted.

Small candles had been carefully placed around the basin's edge in red glass sconces, lit already, the wicks flickering in the cold, cold air. And candles were also burning above the well, above the carved feathers, which she presumed must have been the sign of the Black Prince.

Flowers had been left here, too. Red roses everywhere.

Thrown around on the ground itself, their velvet petals frozen darkly. The whole scene was shrouded in a strange grey mist floating in thin stringy layers, as if by magic.

Magic.

Was that why her American had wanted to meet here? Was it truly a magical place, like the driver of the motor-taxi had suggested?

Ghosts, hauntings, fairies. And magic.

But such places didn't exist, did they?

Or had her date *made* it magic? Was it a stage-set? With everything elaborately placed about to give this effect? Was this actually a work trip?

Was she being tested in some way? Tested, not to be found wanting? Did her future in America depend on something here, in front of her?

She looked about frantically for clues, for something which linked everything together, but she found nothing.

For the first time she felt doubt, and annoyance. This *was* her day off, after all.

And then, despite time passing uncomfortably slowly, she realised she'd been waiting at the Well for half an hour already. The candles were fast becoming the only real source of light.

The sky overhead was dark with only a few last indigo clouds scudding over a dim crescent moon, and crows were calling to each other through the gloom.

Not a person had come by in all that time.

Creepy.

She'd give it two more minutes. Then she'd have to get back to the station somehow, back to London. There were responsibilities there which couldn't be shirked, which made her feel queasy at being away from King's Cross for too long, especially since all that awful business at Southwark.

A shiver ran down her spine.

Buck up!

It had been madness ever coming.

But then there was a sudden quick sound behind her, a crunch of a twig, a frozen rose stem, perhaps. A tread of a very heavy heel and dense, solid weight hitting ice.

Thank Goodness!

She swirled around, half-thankful, half-angry. Exasperated, for sure, but anxious to seem light-hearted, rescue the situation for her American gentleman.

Perhaps he'd been genuinely held up?

Or maybe, he'd been waiting for precisely the right moment. She had, if she admitted it, in her heart of hearts, been thinking he might propose here.

That would be neat.

At least a diamond ring would make this wretched trip worthwhile, eh?

Sensing rather than seeing the swish of a cape around his bulky form, she took in the outline of his top-hat against the blackness: black on black.

Why on earth was he dressed like that?

She licked her lips.

A half-laugh bubbled up in her throat: 'Is this a new idea for work? For a show for *us*? Should I have worn a stage outfit, too?'

But then, before she could say anything else, she saw a fizz of silver arching through the air, heard the crows above screaming and fluttering in a cacophony of warning.

'Oh! Lawks! What thc…?'

She sensed, too late, that the dark rivers spreading out upon the snow-covered ground, blurring with the rose petals, were made up of her blood, and she realised with a crushing disbelief that the sudden jarring pain in her heart was a knife, a knife she knew well.

And then she was down.

Down.

Down on the ground, her red shoes hammering on the ice.

There were no miracles, no ghosts, no fairies to help her here.

And there was definitely no magic.

As she took her last rasping breath on earth, pinned to the floor by a silver knife which she handled every day, and felt her eyes freeze open in their very last ever act, she thought of diamond rings and New York and the endlessly rising skyscrapers she had pinned to her mirror, which glowed with the romance of the dressing-room, and whose reality she would never see.

'You have taken my dreams away,' she breathed. 'It's murder… And just because of the mirror?'

He loomed over her, stared into her beautiful, one-in-a-million doll-like face.

'*What?*' he demanded, panicky, nettled, on the edge of all reason. 'What did you say, girl? What was that about a *mirror*?'

But there was no reply.

She was already gone.

****

PART ONE
Friday 18th December, 1925
(Bloomsbury, London)

Chapter One

Posie had been gone for a bit.

The howling wind of the Sussex coast had blown away the shadows that had been gathering around her. The salty air had done her good.

And now she was back again, with Christmas – and a long list of things which needed to be done before that festive holiday – lurking uncomfortably just around the corner.

Posie Parker, London's premier female detective, walked into her office and gently closed the door behind her with a soft, satisfying *click*.

A quiet, dead silence hung in the room. A freezing cold surrounded her, as if no-one had been in for ages.

No fire burned in the fireplace and no lamps were lit. A fire was needed in here: today had been icy cold, with the temperature constantly stuck below zero.

She'd stepped onto a lot of letters, and she bent down to gather them all up.

The Detective Agency was located on the top floor of a red-bricked corner building on Grape Street in Bloomsbury, a hidden slice of central London. It was an underrated and slightly grubby area of town which was, however, handy for clients; bordered as it was by the theatre district in Covent Garden, the legal heart of the city at Holborn, the shopping paradise of Oxford Street, and the tourist trap of the British Museum, right around the corner.

Posie walked to the window and pulled up the sash, looking out at the museum, its grey balustrades just visible over the high-up rooftops.

Snowflakes fluttered like soft ash through the blue afternoon sky and Posie took a deep breath of the frozen London air.

It felt good to be back, even if she wasn't planning on being in the office for long.

Posie had decided she would start work again properly after Christmas. She had one big case, an unresolved mystery, waiting nigglingly for her, needing to be addressed, but it would require time and patience, and perhaps weeks of planning, and energy, and a bit of luck.

It was for later.

Now was a time for hunkering down and making meticulous lists, for getting back on top of things.

A time for organising treats and clever, thoughtful presents for the children, and gifts too for darling Richard, whose forty-fifth birthday was next week.

Forty-Five!

Golly, there had been a time, in Posie's twenties, when attaining the age of forty had seemed a milestone so far off that it was almost unspeakable; unfathomable to imagine.

And now here was her own dear Richard, twelve years older than herself, well past that unfathomable age, but looking pretty good on it, actually.

Trim, and gorgeous still.

True, Richard Lovelace's vivid red hair was paler now, greying at the temples, and a slight furrow was etched onto his brow, but his bright green eyes still sparkled mischievously, as if hinting at a shared intrigue. He wore his age like a fine wine, the extra years suiting him, adding extra gravitas to his position as Chief Commissioner of New Scotland Yard.

He was the most senior policeman in the land.

Posie had been very lucky, she knew that: finding Richard; meeting him; marrying him. There were ups and downs of course, and the children they shared between them were both a source of utmost happiness and utmost pain, but most of the time Posie knew she was lucky to have him as her best friend. And by Gad, she loved him.

They were meeting up later tonight for dinner, at Kettner's, Posie's favourite restaurant, for the best fish and chips in town.

She had bought a new jade-green dress with little silver sparkles on it to wear for her return to London, and while it would be ridiculously over the top for a place like Kettner's, she'd get the devil of a kick out of wearing it, and feeling like she was out and about in the world again, that London was hers for the taking again.

Posie grinned as she crossed the waiting room to the secretary's desk, putting down the pile of post, shrugging off her new thick, warm tweed coat with its little attached capelet which Richard said made her look like Sherlock Holmes.

As if!

To have a modicum of the great fictional sleuth's famous detective skills would have come in extremely handy during the four years since she'd set up the Detective Agency.

And although Posie was pretty proud of her record as a detective so far – a glittering string of mostly solved cases, which had sometimes involved famous clients and had therefore been reported on heavily in the newspapers – the last few months had been very sparse. The pickings had become lean.

Letters now crossed Posie's desk which in the past would have been binned immediately by the secretary, Prudence. The appointments diary was pretty much empty.

Posie leant against Prudence's desk and flicked through what had come in today: circulars, mainly, and some office bills. There were a couple of Christmas cards from law firms who liked to stay friendly, with silver-glittered robins and fat curly-haired angels appearing almost sinister in all their forced joviality. There were also some serious-looking letters for Len, Posie's partner at the Detective Agency, but he was away on a big case in Eastbourne, and Posie felt a sharp jolt of jealousy just looking at his stack of post.

'Oh, what I'd give for a real case for *me*!' she muttered crossly, piling the paperwork up again, ready for Prudence to deal with on Monday.

The ever-reliable Prudence had asked for an afternoon off today, starting at noon, which was very unusual, and Posie wondered vaguely what might be afoot.

Posie had flicked on the lamp in her own inner office, and was about to telephone her Christmas food order through to Fortnum's when she heard a rapid hammering at the frosted glass outer door.

Turning, frowning, she saw a man's silhouette out on the landing.

She checked her watch, saw it was not yet three o'clock and remembered the empty diary with no scheduled appointments in it. She strode over, and through the protection of the glass she addressed the man:

'Hello? Who is it?'

'Miss Parker? Miss Posie Parker?'

The man's voice was clipped and clear, but slightly reedy on the edges.

'Ye-es. Can I help you?'

'I hope so. I'm here to see you.'

'Without an appointment?' She felt, and sounded, she supposed, aggravated. But this wasn't the kind of establishment where it was appropriate to turn up uninvited. Besides, she was on her own here, and she guarded her safety above all things.

'I normally only meet clients who contact me in the proper manner.'

Snooty now, slightly bitter. Ridiculous too, really. Speaking to each other between a pane of frosted glass.

The man continued: 'I've been trying to telephone you all morning, or rather, my secretary has. But the Operator couldn't make a connection at this exchange. There was no answer on this line.'

Actually, that made sense – the freezing cold temperature, the post left lying on the mat – these things spoke of an office which had been empty all day.

So where had Prudence been this morning?

Had Prudence been planning on coming in, as she had told Posie she would, for the morning, but then something else had occurred? And was Prudence all right?

Posie couldn't feel anger or disappointment, as she herself had done nothing better with her morning than sit in bed drinking Darjeeling tea and scanning the newspapers. And whilst it was a rare occurrence, an indulgence born as it was on the back of a small holiday, it had made Posie feel guilty nonetheless, snuggled beneath the thick turquoise velvet throw of their ridiculously comfortable bed.

She gritted her teeth, unlocked the door and pulled it open several inches, but left it on the safety chain.

The man outside was lean, finely-built, only about her height. In his mid-twenties, he had probably missed the Great War, lucky blighter. But his presence was quite extraordinary and Posie tried not to stare too overtly.

The man seemed to shimmer in the rays of the light spilling in dust-mote-filled seams onto the shabby landing outside. It was as if he never stood still.

He wore a three-piece suit of periwinkle-blue velvet, with matching blue suede shoes, all exquisitely made. The blue shade was an exact match to the colour of his eyes, but there was something odd about his gaze; it was almost a hypnotic stare. What was it, exactly?

His hair was black and greased back, and his skin was clean-shaven. There was not a hat to be seen, nor an overcoat, despite the freezing cold, and Posie noticed that he wore bright blue satin gloves, which seemed both inappropriate for inside, and insufficient for the weather outside.

But you realised straightaway that this was certainly not a man to be romantic about, or to dream of, even though he dripped wealth and glamour.

He was a sprite, other-worldly, and Posie had the strange sensation of having been visited by some character straight out of a fairy tale, but whether good or bad, she could not yet tell.

'So how can I help you, sir?'

She leant against the door-jamb with one eyebrow raised. She didn't invite him in, or undo the chain on the door.

However, Posie had the feeling, stealing over her, second by second, that she ought to know this man. Was he famous? Some kind of glamour-boy who advertised tea or wool or chocolate in the penny magazines, maybe?

She wished she had kept her Sherlock Holmes coat on; it was nippy out here, and she rather liked the thin veil of authority she felt it gave her.

The man bent down nimbly and started to unzip a bag, which Posie hadn't noticed before as it had been placed behind him on the floor. It too was of a pale sapphire blue, suede, or nubuck leather perhaps; certainly expensive. There was a smidgen of gold embossing at the top of it, but what it was, she couldn't see clearly.

He pulled something out of the bag.

He made a little serious bow, and in his gloved hands were a pair of tickets, black printed words on an unusual snakeskin-embossed gold foil, which must have cost a fortune to print. On closer inspection the pattern was revealed to be tiny golden lions.

'For you, Miss Parker.' The man jittered as he stood there, restless.

Posie took the tickets and read quickly:

INVITATION

The Great COUNT OLLI ONNERI

(Pupil of the Great American Marvel ***HARRY HOUDINI****)*

is playing for ONE SPECIAL NIGHT ONLY at the Holborn Empire, London, WC1.

(To be followed thereafter by a season of three weeks at the Hammersmith Apollo.)

Friday 18th December 1925

7 PM, for a 7.30 PM start

Witness the new and as yet unseen attraction: 'The Magic Mirror!'

At the very bottom was scrawled in black ink: *FRONT ROW PLEASE.*

Posie frowned, then looked up.

'*You're* Count Onneri?'

The man nodded eagerly.

'I've seen your show advertised, of course.'

That much was true. An advert for the Hammersmith run of shows for the New Year had been inside virtually every newspaper and magazine Posie had so much as glanced at in the last month.

She wasn't really into magic shows, if truth be told. But the adverts had featured a caricature of this very man's face, albeit with a trim little black beard in place, and Posie realised this was how she had recognised the man in front of her now. The little caricature had been surprisingly accurate, although it had shown Onneri with a black top hat on, and summoning doves from a hat.

The main thrust of the magazine adverts, however, had been to highlight Onneri's connection to Houdini, whose legendary fame was an easy way to lure in thrill-seeking Londoners, who could never quite get enough of Houdini's exploits, although it seemed like years since he had been in the capital.

But the Onneri shows were achieving quite some buzz in their own right, and the posters pasted up for it at Underground stations all over town always seemed to have a crowd around them. A magical man no-one had ever heard of before certainly seemed to have London all a-twitter.

Thinking about it, Posie was sure Len had booked tickets for one of Onneri's shows and had been chattering about it a couple of weeks ago.

Len.

Handsome Len who she hadn't seen for a couple of weeks now, whose presence in her life was somehow still strangely important: the lover who had never been a lover; the friend who had always been more than a friend; the man who could never, ever have been her husband.

Well, not really.

'Miss Parker?'

'Oh! Sorry…'

The magician was staring at Posie now, half-curiously, and in her slight confusion Posie gabbled, as if coming up for air, focusing on something obvious.

His name. That would do.

'Oliver Onneri? So, you're an Italian?'

The man shrugged pleasantly. 'Perhaps I am. Perhaps I am not. Magic makes the very best of people, don't you think so, Miss Parker?'

'I don't know about that, Count Onneri. I deal in facts. Not magic. I always think of magic as belonging to the night, somehow. And most of my cases need to be examined in the cold, hard light of day. You and I, we belong to different worlds.'

She ventured onto something more certain. 'You worked with Houdini?'

The man's blue hypnotic eyes sparkled. 'That's right. I was fortunate enough to meet him here in England, actually. Spring 1920: when he was starting his big country-wide tour. He took me back to America with him at the end of it all. I learnt great things from him. I had my own shows. I'm truly indebted. I'm only just back here, and I feel it's time to show off some of what I learnt.'

'I see.'

Well, that explained why no-one had ever heard of the man before, Posie supposed, a little begrudgingly.

Posie thought she'd better offer him tea.

She could scratch something together from whatever Prudence and Len had left in the small office kitchen. She hoped there was a bottle of fresh milk out on the window-sill, and if so, that it hadn't frozen up completely. She released the chain and held the door open wider.

'Tea, Count Onneri?' she asked politely, speaking aloud his surname with a slow and dead-pan seriousness, for she was sure, as sure as bread was bread, that the exotic surname and the title he had given himself were both fakes: stage-names.

Lies.

He'd pretty much just admitted that himself.

But no matter: theatre and magic always demanded a certain amplified glamour, even if it was borrowed. She was certain this entertainer was as English as she was. There was not even a trace of an accent here, fake or otherwise.

The Count bowed again. 'I must decline your kind offer of refreshment, Miss Parker. But I thank you. I have to get back to the theatre to set up for tonight.'

'The Holborn Empire? I didn't see this particular show advertised.'

'It *hasn't* been advertised. It's a very special show; a taster, really. I'm not at all familiar with the Holborn Empire. It's normally a variety venue, isn't it?'

'That's right. It's around the corner from here.'

'I've been given the chance to take it over for one night, tonight, for free. The opportunity came up quite unexpectedly, actually. It was last-minute; a cancellation, I think. But it's very exciting. I've invited the press into the first few rows of the stalls; as many journalists as I can find, in the hope of generating interest for the big Apollo shows. I need a big buzz. My secretary and myself have been busy today going all around town dropping off these golden tickets to journalists, and every famous person we can think of. We had them printed up last night. The other seats in the theatre will be allocated on a first-come, first-served basis on the door, but no riff-raff allowed. These golden tickets will be expensive. We've announced the tickets for tonight's show in several newspapers, which should be out on the streets in about one hours' time. I hope people will clamour for them.'

'That's clever. Making it exclusive, special.'

Posie flapped her pair of tickets in the air, frowning slightly.

'But *I'm* not the press. And I'm not that famous. I'm not part of any buzz. Are these really for me?'

Time to be blunt now. 'And if so, *why*? And front-row tickets? How so?'

Count Onneri threw his head back and laughed. His laugh was thin and reedy, and unsurprisingly girlish.

'I like it when people are straight with me. I am asking

you because you *are* famous, Miss Parker. Rightly so. And in my business, fame attracts fame. I have in mind to ask you to come up on stage with me. You see, there is a mirror trick I do… I would invite you up on stage before I do the trick and simply ask you to walk around the back of the mirror and tell my audience that what you find there is a straightforward mirror. Nothing more, nothing less.'

'And *is* that what I would find there? A straightforward, normal mirror?'

Count Onneri grinned, his body moving all the while. 'But of course. So, you will accept tonight's invitation? Plus, you may bring another person with you, of course. Your esteemed policeman husband, perhaps? He's famous, too.'

So, the strange magician had done his homework, then.

Posie felt slightly annoyed: she didn't feel like going to a magic show, still less appearing on stage in one.

In fact, she had been very much looking forward to the meal out, and that was all. Time alone with Richard, and good food. She was always hungry these days. She supposed she was turning into a bit of an old grump.

But then she thought about her depressingly empty in-tray, and her lack of any decent cases at the moment.

And this man was right, fame attracted fame. There would be journalists there tonight, and photographers. And if this man could be so self-serving about his career, surely she could be too?

Perhaps her photograph in the newspapers again might chivvy a few readers into contacting her about some unresolved issue in their own lives: a small mystery which might need solving; a relative who needed to be found?

Besides, there was her beautiful jade-green dress to wear, which undoubtedly demanded some sort of audience and attention.

She would have time to run to her hairdressers if she left now, and have her short dark-brown hair cut sharply and razored into place. Posie planned to wear stacks of pearls, and maybe even a headdress fixed into place with tiny jewelled hairclips. Long white gloves, maybe, if gloves were the "thing" at magic shows these days.

She'd make sure she looked her very best tonight. And heaven knew when there had last been an occasion demanding such glamour.

'Fine. I'll be there.'

'Splendid. Thank you. Perhaps you could come along to my dressing-room before the show starts, Miss Parker? I'll introduce you to my team. You'll need to come to the Stage Door. Oh, er, there is one small item I'd like to ask your opinion about.'

'Oh?'

For the first time Onneri looked slightly uncomfortable. He picked up his big blue duffle bag carefully, his satin gloves slipping slightly against the leather handle, and he seemed to be on the cusp of opening the bag again, but then he hurriedly turned on his heel.

'No, never mind. Until later, then!'

And Posie watched, then heard, him go bounding off down the staircase, light-footed as a mountain-goat on his thin-soled blue shoes.

She went inside again and picked up the telephone apparatus, tapping through to the Operator.

'New Scotland Yard, please.' She wondered what Richard would make of their changed plans for the evening.

Not much, she supposed.

In both their respective lines of work, they dealt with trickery and fakery and fraud every single day. This time it was simply labelled as such.

Magic was just a string of carefully-rehearsed events, prettied up in fancy wrappings.

But who cared?

Besides, it might just be a jolly good show.

****

Chapter Two

The Holborn Empire was close, tucked behind Holborn Underground Station in a slip of a side-road.

It was normally the haunt of working Londoners seeking some light entertainment: comedians, singers, can-can girls in faded skirts and boas shedding feathers everywhere.

Usually, the outside stonework looked grey and grubby, but tonight special care had been taken and gold, glittering sequin-embellished banners with foot-high black letters spelling out the words 'MAGIC' and 'ONNERI' were trailing down the sides of the building, and impressive beacons were already blazing at the doorway itself.

Crowds of London's poorest children in threadbare rags were gathering near the beacons, trying to get warm, and policemen waving truncheons were darting this way and that, breaking up these little groups.

To the far left, and by contrast, a dense crowd of quite well-dressed men and women in thick dark coats queued, some clutching their golden tickets, others jostling to get to the very small box office window to try and buy theirs, despite a 'SOLD OUT' notice already perched in the tiny barred window.

Some motor-cars had already parked up on the kerb of

High Holborn, and Posie noticed out of the corner of her eye that the cars were mainly full of journalists, and their trench-coat-wearing colleagues, the photographers, were already loading up flashbulbs and searching for a good shot, even while still inside the cars.

Tonight had all the makings of a London sensation.

They were starting to take shots of the queues of well-dressed Londoners, and also of the pathetically cold street children; of their starved faces lit up beneath the shimmering golden sequins.

The bright lights of the flashbulbs were becoming an amusement in their own right, and the street children started to run up to the cars, shouting out for money, banging on the windows.

Richard muttered at Posie in an undertone: 'I don't want to get involved in all this ruckus out here with these poor cold mites. By Gad, it makes my heart bleed. I'll leave them and all the law enforcement to these capable bobbies. And I don't want to get nabbed by one of the hacks out here either. I've already seen your pal Sam Stubbs. Stage Door, didn't you say, darling?'

'What? Oh… oh, yes.'

'Over there. Down that grotty alleyway. Watch where you put your feet. It's so icy. And keep bally well moving along, especially if you suddenly feel hands grabbing at your coat. There are big crowds of seasoned beggars here. Don't get your bag out, let alone open it.'

Richard, who was wearing a huge dark tweed overcoat with the collar well turned up, and his usual homburg hat, steered Posie past the thick of a crowd of beggars, and they turned left smartly, down a tiny lane behind the Empire itself. A green illuminated sign ahead read 'STAGE DOOR' and they marched along towards it, hurrying past a few dark figures who seemed to melt out of the blackness of the brick walls themselves, rustling and whining and moaning, and pleading.

'Givvus a hot meal, Mister… Spare a penny for a poor man?'

Richard ignored this all and banged on the Stage Door.

Posie was next to him, already opening her clip-top silver leather handbag, clicking open her purse inside and dragging out a handful of small change, and she threw it on the frozen floor behind her in a glittering arc as the door ahead was opened to them.

Richard exhaled in disbelief and shook his head but within seconds they were standing inside a narrow hallway with peeling floral wallpaper and a tattered scarlet carpet, all illuminated with a single bright overhead bare bulb.

The suffocating stink of sweat and greasepaint hit them hard.

A small, exceedingly slight young woman in a deep purple suit with gold buttons in a prominent row on the jacket had opened the door. She was clutching a clip-board and appeared to be nervous; in fact, her hand with a pencil in it looked as if it was shaking.

Posie edged past Richard's bulk.

'I'm Posie Parker,' she stated. 'And this is my husband, Richard Lovelace. Count Onneri is expecting me.'

'Ah, ah yes. I see.'

The woman in purple, who looked no more than eighteen years old, peered at them uncertainly. She was an odd sight, with bulbous light green eyes, set very far apart, and a strange manner of staring fixedly ahead of herself, and Posie wondered if the girl might need strong glasses. Her small face was round and plain with not a bit of make-up on it, her mouth crowded with teeth rather suited for someone much bigger, and she had a very long, almost regal neck. Her sparse short brown hair was greased back in wet, waxy waves over her head, as was becoming the fashion for followers of the dancer of the moment, Josephine Baker.

It was an unfortunate choice in this case. She looked

like a particularly toothy long-necked toad, wet from the pond.

But the slip of a girl attempted a smile. 'I'm Miss Peterson, the secretary.'

Surprisingly, the girl had an unexpectedly lovely voice, low and rich, quite commanding. It was by far her best asset. 'What an honour to have you both here with us tonight. Please follow me.'

And then they traipsed down a steep staircase into the very bowels of the building, and on through a rabbit-warren of passageways, stinging with the scent of damp, and all at once they came upon people milling about in a very brightly-lit corridor: a big, burly, bearded man with a length of thick metal chains coiled heavily in his arms, checking all the links, and a small, buxom, cheaply-beautiful blonde girl of about twenty with thick red glitter paste on her eyes and even thicker face make-up, wearing what looked like a red ballerina's tutu, applying false lashes in a compact mirror.

Neither of the pair greeted Posie or Richard, but concentrated intently on their tasks at hand.

Two or three doors were open along here, each marked 'DRESSING-ROOM'. But two were marked 'OUT OF USE' and there was only one door with lights on inside, showing under the door.

Miss Peterson went up to the door and she rapped. 'Count Onneri? Your guests are here for you.'

There was a rustle, as of crepe paper, and the door to the dressing-room was flung open.

The man from earlier stood in front of Posie and Richard, and he made a sweeping gesture welcoming them both inside.

They trooped in, and the scent of chalk and dust and sweat and greasepaint was stronger than ever in here. This was a large room, obviously intended for use by maybe three performers.

A vanity table, like a bench, ran the full length of the room on the right-hand side, with a long continuous mirror placed above it, framed by bright electric light-bulbs all the way around. But the two spaces further towards the wall were unoccupied, the chairs empty.

'Welcome! Welcome! I hope Miss Peterson has offered you some champagne?'

'Sorry? Oh, no. No, I don't want any, but thank you. Richard?'

Richard shook his head and tried to look as if he was taking everything very seriously.

Posie tried not to stare. Yes: it *was* the same man from earlier, only now Count Onneri had actually *become* his caricature.

The black hair was powdered blacker, a fake black beard had been applied, quite convincingly actually, and the man's eyebrows and eyelashes had been accentuated with thick black greasepaint. His face was chalk-white with powder and he was already wearing the black magician's hat featured in all the advertisements, and a black tuxedo. He wore the same or an identical pair of royal-blue satin gloves as he had worn earlier. A black cape rustled about him as he dragged two stools over to his end of the long vanity table.

Photographs and ancient head-shots of actors and actresses who had occupied this room were pasted up around the mirror like an extra frame among the pearly bright bulbs. Most of the pictures were curling up in the damp of the air.

Posie caught sight of images of a few actors and actresses who had been well known before the Great War, but whose stars had fizzled out long ago into obscurity. A postcard of New York was taped up among the head-shots, the Woolworth Building standing proudest and tallest among a clutch of skyscrapers, with words in burgundy lipstick underneath saying 'TEN DAYS TO GO!'

Posie found herself turning in fascination, observing the blooms of green mould on every surface, the mess of damp cardboard boxes stacked up against the walls, all overflowing with long-unused wigs and bits of moth-eaten animal-fur pelts.

Her attention was dragged back to her host's voice:

'Do sit. Excuse the dressing-room, won't you? We are, after all, only here for one night. I am not in permanent residence.'

It was freezing down here, and Posie gathered her too-thin black opera coat all around her. Both she and Richard kept their gloves and hats and scarves on as they sat down rather awkwardly.

Posie looked into the mirror. Reflected in it was a medium-sized wooden cabinet, right behind her. It was out of the ordinary, even here.

Turning, she saw it was the size of a bread-oven, and it was bolted tight to the wall. It had a strange burnt pattern down its open door, where the varnish had been stripped away violently, and a series of perhaps twenty tiny intricate locks running down the side of the open door.

Inside, the cabinet appeared to be empty, except for maybe one crispy, curling piece of paper on the bottom shelf.

But the jolly odd thing was right *beside* the cabinet. Ancient graffiti.

Painted onto the wall alongside was a big black arrow pointing inwards to the cupboard, and the words 'PROPERTY OF RICKY DI MAGGIO – DON'T TOUCH OR HOUDINI OR I WILL DARN WELL PUT A SPELL ON YOU! OR WORSE!'

She turned back and caught Onneri's strange blue gaze suddenly, in the mirror. Saw that he, too, had been staring fixedly at the cabinet, and that his pupils were strangely dilated and massive, very noticeable in the bright lights here.

He looked a little paler behind his make-up than

before, his hands trembled and his rustling cape was like something alive.

Posie was intrigued.

Why is he so uncomfortable here? It's as if he's seen a ghost!

The magician forced a laugh now, rescuing the situation: 'I hope my dressing-room at the Apollo will be a little more salubrious than this one! Although finding Houdini's name here does seem like some kind of good luck charm!'

'Was Houdini ever here, do you know, Count Onneri?' asked Posie politely.

The man laughed rather dismissively. 'I don't think so. He liked nice glossy places. This is decidedly down at heel. All this old rubbish lying about...I feel a little spooked, to be honest.'

It was true that this was an odd place. A film of grot and grime was everywhere, along with these strange preserved memories, creepy shadows of former occupants, their ghostly messages speaking out across the years.

The surface of the vanity table they sat at was, however, meticulously clean and clear, and Posie could see that Count Onneri's own effects, his own make-up, had already been stashed away in a neat blue leather vanity bag, which was left open. A tiny golden lion had been printed on the bag, with a small interlocking double initial of 'OO' beside it. It was ostentatious, but charming.

He was obviously ready for his show.

'You're still all right to come on stage?' He smiled cheerily.

Posie nodded. 'Of course. I'm rather looking forward to it.'

'Good. So, I'll announce you, and you come up straightaway. All you have to do is attest to the audience that what you are looking at on stage is a perfectly normal mirror.'

Richard, who had said nothing so far, laughed good-naturedly. 'I take it that the mirror is anything *but* a perfectly normal mirror, Count Onneri?'

Onneri tapped his nose with a blue satin finger in a confidential 'you-may-never-know' gesture. 'I am lucky enough to have an excellent technical director, Matt Jenkins – you may have seen him outside just now, testing out my props? – and he is particularly skilled at creating perfectly normal items. Perfectly normal for magic shows, that is.'

Lovelace laughed again.

'Quite. Well, if that is all, Count Onneri, my wife here and I will go upstairs to the bar. To drink a quick something before your show.'

Richard needs to get warm, thought Posie. *To get away from this dreadful underground hole.*

They both stood up, but Onneri remained in his seat, staring blankly ahead in the mirror. 'You must get upstairs, of course. Only...'

As one, Richard and Posie turned and stared at the magician. He was holding his black satin hat in his blue-gloved hands very formally, looking slightly less confident than before.

'Count Onneri? Is there something else?' Posie dropped her voice, and sensed rather than saw Richard closing the dressing-room door behind them, a move designed to blot out the potential eavesdropping of the people in the corridor. Richard stayed well back, leaning against the door.

Posie carried on, tentatively: 'Is there something you haven't yet spoken of, sir? Something you are worried about, perhaps?'

The made-up magician blew out his cheeks, slightly embarrassed, put down his hat, and began to delve within his open blue make-up case. He picked up an object which was perfectly normal to find there.

A mirror.

Onneri held it gingerly in his gloved hands, as if it might ignite.

It was a mirror with a handle, the face of it the size of

a small saucer. The casing was standard and non-descript; some sort of cheap bronze-coloured metal with a scrollwork design moulded all over it.

It was the sort of thing every girl in England owned; a mirror you could pick up on the Woolworths counter for a few pennies. The kind you could buy together with a matching hairbrush and comb. Although the style of this one was slightly dated.

You wouldn't have glanced twice at the thing, but then Onneri turned it around, so the face of it flashed fully at both Posie and Richard.

Posie gasped and she heard Richard move quickly behind her. He joined her immediately, right at her side.

The word 'MURDER' had been scrawled right across the mirror's face in jagged capital letters.

'I say!' whispered Posie. 'Did someone send this to you? Or did you simply find it here? In this dressing-room?'

'Both,' answered the magician, sounding uncomfortable. 'As I said to you, Miss Parker, when I visited your office earlier, we are only playing here at the Holborn Empire for one evening, and it is an unexpected honour. But this was waiting for me here, in this dressing-room this morning, and it was packaged up in tissues within a cake-box from a bakery in Piccadilly, with my name and this theatre's address written upon it. Needless to say, there were no cakes in the box. And the bakery in question, Fritzi's, is no more: it went out of business some years ago. I should know; I went to the location myself today and asked all about. My secretary, Miss Peterson, opened this package in all innocence this morning and then screamed her head off. I can tell you, she's been spooked ever since. Shaking, trembling.'

'Ah, understandably.'

The magician swallowed uneasily. 'I wrestled the thing off her, and had a good look. It looks like the actual glass of the mirror has been etched into with something: acid, perhaps? It's created very sharp edges, whatever was used. I cut myself slightly on the jagged edges of the surface when I grabbed it from my secretary.'

He tapped at the third finger of his right hand, encased in its blue satin glove. 'I *was* going to mention it to you earlier, Miss Parker. I had wrapped the mirror up carefully and I'd brought it with me in my bag, but I thought better of showing it to you at your offices, Miss Parker. I lost my nerve at the last minute.'

He probably thought I wouldn't come, or at least I wouldn't agree to take part in a magic show involving a mirror, if he showed me such a horrid thing, thought Posie ruefully.

Lovelace stepped forward. 'Let's take a look, sir,' he said calmly, as if he was asking to view a particularly interesting cat or dog, and Onneri placed the mirror into Richard's leather-gloved hands.

Lovelace turned it this way and that in the strange bright light of the dressing-room. He sniffed at it several times, nodded, satisfied.

Onneri gnawed at his lip.

'What do you think, Inspector?'

Lovelace shrugged easily.

'Must be some loony with too much time on their hands,' he said, calmly. 'I come across a good deal of such filth being sent to well-known performers. It's very sad. Have you encountered something like this before in your career, sir?'

Count Onneri shook his head sadly. 'I've only been working in America, Inspector,' he replied. 'For my entire career so far. I never got as much as a cross word, let alone anything in the mail. The audiences were well-behaved and very polite.'

'Lucky you.'

But Posie sensed there was more. 'How long *have* you been back in England, Count Onneri? Has anything else odd occurred?'

Silence.

Richard put the mirror down carefully on the floor and stepped away from it.

'My wife has asked a jolly good question, Onneri. Has anything else like this message been sent your way?'

The magician paused, fiddled with the fake black beard, patting at it, checking its dried-on glue.

'I've been back since the end of November, a total of twenty-two days. In that time I have assembled my little British team, apart from Matt, of course: he's American and I brought him back with me from America. Other than him, there's just my stage assistant, and my secretary. You've seen them; they were all out in the corridor. We've been preparing for the show at the Hammersmith Apollo religiously. We've been staying at the Ritz, in a suite on the top floor. And every single day I've received something weird.'

'Go on,' said Richard. But any previous humour in his voice was absent now, and Posie knew he was switching up into work mode, and quickly.

The big duffle bag from earlier was being hauled up onto a stool, and Count Onneri was pulling lots of identical small things out of it, quickly, nimbly.

Close to it now, Posie noticed the small golden lion and the interlocking 'OO' as a now-familiar motif. Perhaps Onneri had this embossed on everything he owned?

The items being pulled out were wrapped in white tissue, which Onneri was now ripping away, throwing the flimsy paper to the floor like inconvenient, irrelevant confetti, placing the unwrapped items on the dressing-table. One item placed after another, all in a meticulous, careful row.

Like a trick. But without any magic.

'Let me show you. This is the order in which I received these things...'

After a minute he was finished, and Posie and Richard peered down.

Twenty-two jagged little pieces of egg-sized mirror were placed in a line, each one roughly the same size, all of them dangerously sharp at the edges. Lethal. All of them etched into with a single letter.

The row, together, spelled out a message:

M U R D E R

T H R O U G H

T H E

M I R R O R

'How exceedingly lovely,' said Posie, calmly.

In truth, she didn't know what to say. She was on the verge of thinking the showman in front of her was making it all up.

It all seemed too fantastical, too timely, too of a piece with a man attempting to garner attention and publicity before a big run of shows.

Did Onneri think Posie would go to the London press with this story, or claim it as a 'case' for herself, similarly securing attention?

Richard however was standing calmly observing the letters, as if he gave them and their sinister message a real significance.

He didn't touch them this time. He kept looking over at Onneri's make-up bag with a quizzical, interested eye.

Lovelace looked up briefly. 'Onneri, tell me: is there any way in which this perfectly normal mirror of yours in the show tonight could bally well be tampered with? Made lethal? Made into an instrument of murder?'

'No, Inspector. Not at all.'

'Fine. Do you have any enemies, Onneri?'

'None, sir.'

'And your team, you're certain of them all? None of them are rotten apples? It's not an inside thing designed to make you nervous?'

The magician laughed but there wasn't any mirth in it.

'No. Matt Jenkins and I go a long way back: years. And I'm married to my stage assistant, Thelma; the Countess Onneri. And my secretary, Miss Peterson, well, she's a relative of Harry Houdini himself, and he asked me to take her on as a favour to him. None of them are behind this. I guarantee it.'

'A loony mad fan then, looking for attention.' Richard swallowed slightly uneasily.

'Well, I wouldn't worry too much, Onneri. If your on-stage mirror is as you described it to me, how can anything go wrong? And if you *do* have any concerns, I'll be sitting in the front row. Just shout.'

Posie stared at her husband in disbelief.

She couldn't understand Richard's glibness, unless he too thought this was all a piece of showmanship and attention-seeking? But she was sure she'd sensed a touch of real unease in her husband's manner just then, before Richard had fobbed the magician off with his platitudes.

Was Richard masking his concerns for some reason she was not yet privy to?

But Count Onneri seemed convinced and slightly happier. He put his black hat on again and checked a small silver pocket-watch on a chain.

'We'll leave you to it, then,' declared Richard cheerily. 'Best of luck tonight.'

'Thank you, Inspector. I'm hoping I don't need it!'

That thin, reedy laugh again.

Out in the corridor only the beautiful young blonde woman in the red tutu was left, her back to them, concentrating, crunching her sandalled feet over and over again into a box of crackling rosin, much like ballerinas did to avoid slipping on polished floors.

Hadn't Onneri just said she was his *wife*? Thelma, the Countess Onneri?

Or had Posie misheard? Got it wrong?

But the woman in red had been the only other woman in the corridor earlier, and she fitted the description of being a stage assistant.

The woman jumped out of the box suddenly and turned, and Posie almost banged right into her. The woman yelled: 'Lawks! Wotch it, won't ya?'

The two women were so close together that Posie could see the thin strips of black bruises covering her cheeks and neck, thickly covered in orange panstick. The woman stared at Posie in a hostile manner, flashed dark eyes warily, her chin raised in a challenging way.

'I'm so sorry,' Posie mumbled, edging away.

'You'd better wotch yer dainty little step, lovey,' the young woman called out in an unmistakably cockney voice, rough at the edges with years of heavy smoking. But there was a terrible fragility there too, which was awful to behold.

'Oh, I will watch my step,' muttered Posie to herself as she hurried back up the corridor, following Richard.

What a dreadful place, she thought to herself.

And what a jolly strange lot of people.

'Inspector? Miss Parker? You're heading upstairs?'

The ugly goblin-like secretary in purple appeared suddenly before them, pulling aside a thick, stained baize curtain set into an alcove of the corridor.

'You can go up here! It's a staircase leading right up to the Stalls. The exit into the theatre is partly-concealed at the top by a black gauze curtain. I think this route up is normally used by cigarette-girls and ice-cream sellers during the intervals. It's all a bit dirty, but much easier for you than going outside again. It's probably quicker, and warmer. See you later, I hope. For the after-party, in the bar?'

'Sorry, what? Oh, yes. I hope so. Thank you.'

Posie and her husband were alone at last on the narrow uncarpeted staircase, in the dim grey light filtered down from the black gauze curtain up ahead.

'We're getting out of here as soon as the show is over, Posie,' said Richard in an undertone, leading the way. 'There's no after-party for us, I'm afraid.'

'Fine by me. I'm starving: Kettner's were jolly nice about giving us a later table but I want to eat something *now*. Goodness, it's all pretty wierd here, isn't it? That woman in the red tutu - Thelma - did Onneri say she was his *wife*? Well, that can't be right, can it? They make an odd pair. Besides, a man like Onneri wouldn't have married. Not her, not any woman. And he said he'd only been in England for twenty-two days; in which time he'd assembled a team. *She* certainly didn't come from America, did she? So has he married Thelma during these past twenty-two days, as part of assembling his team?'

'I don't think much is standard here, darling. Perhaps she's simply a stage-wife? Akin to a stage-name, you know: all a lot of hot air.'

'And did you see her face?'

'I tried not to look too hard.'

'You should have done, Richard. It was a mass of bruises. The cream panstick she'd applied was to disguise the marks. The false eyelashes and red glitter were covering a black eye.'

'By Gad, how sad. A short marriage, eh? But a bad one, it seems. So Onneri is not quite the squeaky-clean bit of magical stardust he makes out to be, eh? What a surprise!'

They reached the top of the stairs and looked out over the theatre from behind the thin, translucent curtain.

The Holborn Empire was packed full, and smartly-dressed people were standing in the aisles, chatting, holding glasses. The press pack were grouped together at the front, chattering away like hyenas, right up near the stage.

Fortunately, it was much warmer up here and Posie slipped off her coat.

'I've got a telephone call to make, darling,' said Richard, scanning the huge theatre through the curtain. He was obviously looking for the exit to the foyer. 'You go and sit down. I'll join you in a minute or so with drinks.'

'Fine.'

'Oh, and, Posie sweetheart? You didn't bally well touch that first mirror, did you?'

Posie noticed how her husband was carefully peeling off his tan leather gloves. He placed them gingerly into his coat pocket.

'No. I looked, but only from afar. *You* were the one who took the mirror.'

She was surprised, and it must have shown on her face.

'I'm getting a call placed to Poots and the Forensics boys at the Yard. I want them over here as soon as bally possible. That chappie Onneri was right about the word on the mirror being etched with acid, but the etching was loaded up with something grimmer: I'm sure of it. I didn't want to panic the lad, though. Not before a show.'

'Oh? Not blood or something awful?'

'A poison, so yes: something awful. But I can't be sure of *what* type of poison exactly. I'm imagining strychnine, as it was odourless, but it was definitely white, and slightly crystalline. It was packed into the recesses made by the acid, and I'd bet my hat on the fact that those twenty-two small shards of mirror are laced with the same stuff, too. It's a bally miracle the man's still alive, especially if he *did* cut himself on the finger today. It must have been just a little graze.'

Posie exhaled sharply: 'Strychnine is lethal, isn't it?'

'Too right, Posie darling. Any sort of ingestion, even if he'd touched the stuff then rubbed his eye or his mouth, would have been fatal. Lucky for him that he wears those ridiculous blue gloves, eh? Fella's a bally lucky man, that's all I'll say… That, or crazed on seeking attention. At present I couldn't tell you which. I'll start investigating but I'm not going to hold up his show: we'll look into it properly afterwards.'

'Mnnn. You don't think it was just sugar crystals you saw? That it's all some elaborate hoax or stunt so that we run around, exactly as we are doing, garnering more publicity for him and the show?'

'Doubt it. And if it is, the man's more talented as a showman than I currently give him credit for.'

'But *he* must have seen the white crystals, too? Why didn't he mention them?'

Richard laughed knowingly. 'I suspect the fella sniffs cocaine. Very regularly, and huge amounts. He's certainly jittery enough, and he's full of an inflated confidence which might be the effects of the drug itself. And did you see his eyes, my love? He has constantly dilated pupils, which you may have noticed?'

'Yes. I noticed that properly tonight.'

'Well, that's a typical thing with serious cocaine addicts. Perhaps he regularly gets a powdery film of cocaine over all his things, before tidying up meticulously? Maybe he *did* notice the white powder on the hand-mirror, but wondered if he himself had caused it, and he didn't want to highlight the fact for fear of getting himself into trouble with me. *If* he noticed it at all, that is…'

'Mnnn. Should I be worried, do you think, going up on stage?'

Richard Lovelace paused for a second, then shook his head.

'No. But by Gad, don't touch anything, and keep your distance from Onneri himself.'

'I've got gloves in my bag, nice fancy satin evening ones; not my usual woollen outside ones from earlier. I'll wear those, shall I?'

'Yes, good idea. I think the fella is facing something

dangerous, but it's a slow, calculated campaign of hatred or madness, rather than an elaborate stunt for attention in front of an audience. It will all be fine, darling. I'm going to get Sergeant Fox over here though, anyhow: I think the lad is on night-duty at Scotland Yard tonight and it should only take him ten minutes to arrive in a motor. I'll get anyone else I can muster, too. It never hurts to have a bit of backup round the place, eh?'

But who was he reassuring, Posie wondered.

Himself?

And Posie had a sinking feeling in her stomach as she headed for her seat, and she found that, quite suddenly, the thought of Kettner's made her feel utterly sick.

In fact, she had absolutely no appetite at all.

****

Chapter Three

Posie was thinking about mirrors as the bell was ringing for the show to begin, with Richard's seat still empty beside her in the front row.

Mirrors.

Well, mirrors were always odd things, weren't they? And there had always been myths and eerie folklore surrounding them.

She was currently reading her little stepdaughter Phyllis a most bizarre tale involving a girl called Alice who stepped into a mirror, entering a realm of dark fantasy.

Mirrors.

One of Posie's earliest memories was of her own mother, a woman who had been a mystery in her own right, dropping a mirror and then screaming out that she would have seven years of bad luck: Posie had crawled under her bed, terrified.

And Posie remembered her beloved older brother, Richard Parker, who had died in the Great War. She remembered back to when he was ten or eleven, just arrived home for the Easter holidays from boarding school. He'd been accompanied by a gaggle of friends, who had all teased Posie and tried to make her scared out of her wits by telling her they were trying to conjure up the devil himself by lining up two mirrors perfectly.

She'd got her brother in a heap of trouble that day, ratting on him to their father, who, as a strict and rigorously correct English clergyman, couldn't have imagined any worse behaviour in his children.

Her brother's school friends had been sent home immediately and poor Richard Parker had spent his holidays in a kind of subdued disgrace, confined to his bedroom.

Even now Posie felt a flush of shame creep across her face at her long-ago tittle-tattling, and at the memory of the sad ruin of her brother's precious time at home.

If only they had known how limited all their earthly time together would be, how those long-ago days were actually the most carefree they would ever spend.

Perhaps Posie wouldn't have ratted?

Perhaps her father would have been more lenient?

Perhaps her brother would have had the best school holiday of his short life?

But then, hindsight was a wonderful thing.

And it was hardly ever helpful.

Suddenly loud music and drumming started up from a band in the pit below the stage, and people all around Posie were settling themselves into their seats, laughter dying down quickly as the lights dimmed.

Posie wondered how successful Onneri had been in his quest to get famous people along tonight: she thought she'd seen Genevieve Townsend, the film star, and also Gladys Hamer, the well-known stage actress flitting among the front row, but perhaps it had just been a trick of the light?

After all, most famous people were booked up weeks in advance. Trying to secure their attendance on the day of an event was breathtakingly daring, or cheeky, whichever way you looked at it.

A girl in white was up on the stage, sprinkling powdered rosin in front of the curtains, and for a mad moment Posie thought it was Miss Peterson, in the way she moved, the curve of the long neck, but when the girl turned for a second Posie saw she was a different sort entirely. Lovely, but knowing; sly, even. Dark lipstick immaculate.

A theatre employee, probably the girl from the box office, making herself useful at several of the jobs which needed attending to. A very pretty dogsbody.

Posie watched the girl disappear off between the curtains, but her thoughts were still arcing back to the theme of mirrors.

Mirrors capturing likenesses, a truth.

Or other things, too?

Deeper things, deeper feelings.

Posie remembered back to around this time of year: Christmas, 1917.

She'd been an ambulance driver out on the Western Front, in those dreadful days of the Great War, and one particularly terrible day stood out starkly.

Her own team had lost their 'twin' or counterpart ambulance, and the hideous news had come in while everyone was stuffing down a hurried supper in the Mess Hut attached to their Field Hospital.

The twin ambulance had been blown up, literally, going over a hidden mine, and all of its crew, medics, stretcher-bearers, and even the dog, were dead.

Whatever was left of them was slowly being brought back to the huts.

A nurse, a new addition, only stationed at the Field Hospital for a couple of days, had suddenly gone berserk and stood up from the bench, gripping it, as if she might be in labour, howling aloud. She was Irish, and people started to whisper between themselves that her name was Roisin McCarthy.

Word got out quickly that her fiancé, a stretcher-bearer, also Irish, from their hometown, also just assigned to the Field Hospital so as to be alongside her, had been among the crew, and a hushed silence fell.

Everyone stared down at the table in front of them, respectful of the exercising of grief, however that came.

Roisin had started screaming: 'The mirrors! The mirrors!'

She'd then started ripping off her apron, her white nurse's headdress, grabbing up napkins from all the tables, any fabric she could find, and then she was running along the far wall of the hut, where a series of perhaps fifteen small square mirrors punctuated the flimsy bare wooden walls, lending the dark room a little light.

Roisin had frantically tried to cover each mirror with whatever material she had to hand, running backwards and forwards from the table to get more and more linen.

Benny, Posie's own stretcher-bearer, had muttered into his soup: 'Isn't that only done at a real wake? When there's a body lyin' in the room itself? To let the soul get out? So it doesn't look itself in the mirror and get confused, eh? But there's no body lyin' here, is there? Her poor boyo's still out in the field, more than likely, in smithereens. So why does she bother?'

Andrew Hadley, a ridiculously young doctor, also new to the Front, was sitting further down, and he whispered softly, surprisingly: 'Maybe she's afraid her own soul might be lost too, tonight? And those mirrors will give her that truth.'

It was a conversation Posie had never forgotten, especially as both Benny and Andrew Hadley had later died in the Great War themselves.

The truth.

Well, truth was as difficult a concept as beauty. It lay in the eye of the beholder. Truth was what you could make of it: how you bent the facts to suit yourself.

And magic was also about bending facts; distorting the truth so much that you tricked the observer out of any pre-conceived ideas of the truth they might have.

What on earth was the significance of mirrors in this case?

Why was someone – *if anyone*, because Posie still half-believed Onneri was behind the whole thing himself – sending messages to the magician using mirrors?

What had he done, if anything, to provoke someone into sending those awful, vivid messages?

But darling Richard was sitting down beside her in the darkness of the front row, his familiar lemony scent, which was actually Penhaligon's 'Blenheim Bouquet', of great reassurance to her now, and Posie saw that the curtains were being yanked open, and Onneri was up on the stage, standing in the bright limelight to the accompaniment of much clapping, a wand held aloft, his cape swirled behind him in a magnificent arc.

He looked surprisingly impressive.

No words were spoken at all by Onneri, only the music played, which seemed to change up a gear into *a can-can* tempo, getting louder and louder and louder.

There were doves flying up from his hat, and a shower of golden confetti, pouring like a rain down from the roof of the theatre, falling upon everyone below.

A man's voice offstage, deep and American, announced excitedly:

'THE ONE-AND-ONLY COUNTESS ONNERI WILL NOW JOIN HER HUSBAND ON STAGE FOR THE MOST DARING TRICKS YET SEEN IN LONDON!'

The blonde woman called Thelma, with the thick make-up, Onneri's rather improbable wife, appeared, prancing onto the stage, grinning and pouting, posing in the scarlet tutu. And then, to the beat of a fast drum, seemingly before the audience's very eyes, her clothes were whipped away from her body by Onneri's wand, all in a swirling rush of net and tulle.

She became a whirl of giddy colour-changing tutus: scarlet becoming blue, blue becoming white, white becoming black, black becoming purple, purple becoming green.

Green becoming yellow.

Colours like bruises changing before your eyes.

Posie bit at her lip, staring.

Loud cheers met Thelma's performance, and now bright yellow birds were flying everywhere, and the Countess was stepping backwards, gamely allowing Onneri to pin her by arms and ankles to a huge upright wooden wheel, as big as a motor-car, painted in a ring of giddying colours.

The Count sprang backwards and spun the wheel around, with his wife upon it, and the woman in bright yellow and the coloured painted rings became a blur, while a loud drumming of cheers and clapping stormed the auditorium.

And then the magician stepped near to the wings and put his hand out as the big American, Matt, handed knives across to Onneri. There was a flash of white in the wings and then Matt was gone.

Onneri started to throw the knives as his wife span on the wheel: one after another, after another, after another, all accompanied by a pounding drumming from the music-pit. The blue-gloved hands moving like lightning, the silver of the metal flashing, the wheel turning.

Bang, bang, bang.

The knives hit the spinning wheel with a startling accuracy. Posie hid her eyes behind her hands anyhow. She couldn't bear the suspense.

She heard Richard mutter beside her: 'By Gad! The fella's deranged! But a bally good shot, eh?'

And then the magician brought the wheel to a halt, and posed beside it, with his wife still pinioned upon it, breathless but unhurt, smiling that rictus-like grin, and the theatre auditorium was ablaze with the lights from hundreds of flashes as journalists and photographers rose to their feet as one.

The drumming stopped.

The curtains closed quite suddenly, and there was

silence for a minute as people sat back down, in a frenzy of anticipation.

When the curtains opened again, there was no music this time, but the magician stepped forward and gave a low bow.

'I am Olli Onneri, and I thank you for coming here tonight,' Onneri announced, his voice impressively reaching to the rafters. 'I learnt this next trick from my old boss, Mr Houdini...'

There was a storm of clapping, and cheering, and feet being stamped, and then a breathless silence.

Still no music.

Posie watched as her husband sat silent all through the next trick, which involved heavy iron chains being tied around Count Onneri by the American, Matt Jenkins.

A seemingly impossible escape followed, amid a good deal of hearty applause.

'MORE! MORE!' yelled the crowd. To the side of them Posie was aware of quite a bit of extra movement but the darkness fully obscured it.

The curtains closed again momentarily, and Posie glanced at Richard, who took her hand and squeezed it. 'I'm here,' he hissed. 'As are some of my chaps.'

Posie peered way along the row, beyond her husband, to the very edge of the theatre walls.

She saw the familiar figure of Inspector Oats. He was an old acquaintance, with whom she shared a somewhat chequered history, and she noted he was standing formally, arms crossed, perching against a great faux-marble pillar, his eyes roving the crowds ceaselessly, looking for trouble.

And closer at hand, sitting immediately behind them, was the very blonde Sergeant Fox, smart but inconspicuous in a thick black suit, and along one seat again, Inspector Rainbird, in a grubby grey trench-coat which simply shouted aloud 'POLICEMAN'. The Scotland Yard men must have booted out some of the journalists and taken their seats instead.

She must be on soon?

Posie grabbed her small glittery silver bag and quickly applied some dark-red lipstick, pressing her lips together tightly, anticipating her entrance. She pulled on her white satin elbow-length gloves and smoothed them out.

And all in a rush the curtains were opening, and Posie heard her name being called and she was standing calmly, shimmering up onto the stage in her beautiful jade dress and turning, posing, smiling out at the audience, screwing her eyes up with her white-gloved hand, shielding her face in the light of a hundred flashbulbs.

Her feet crunched the rosin of the boards.

Onneri was introducing Posie.

But she only heard snatches, her eyes searching for and catching onto Richard's green steely gaze; searching out Sergeant Fox; taking in Sam Stubbs of the *Associated Press* a few rows behind, with his surprised grin and cheery thumbs-up.

She heard snippets of her own introduction: 'Miss Posie Parker… Honoured to have her here with us… London's most famous detective, not to mention the most beautiful. A woman who solves every case she takes on with style and finesse! I am lucky she has agreed to help me here tonight.'

Onneri was pulling something out from behind Posie's ear now, a red carnation, then a tiny golden bird, which flew upwards into the audience to the sound of screams and applause.

She noticed Onneri's eyes were particularly bright up on stage, the pupils enormous and almost obliterating the colour of his irises, and two patches of bright red burned on Onneri's cheeks above the fake beard, as if he had a sudden fever.

She had felt how violently his hands were shaking inside their blue gloves as he had handed her the red carnation.

Posie now felt his gloved hand in her satin-encased one, and together they stepped to the very centre of the stage, about a metre back from the edge, where a bright round spotlight was focused. Gold-sequined curtains glimmered at the back of the set.

And in the very centre of the beam of bright white light was a mirror, about an inch or so thick, and about seven or eight feet high, with plain wooden piping all around it like a frame. It stood on two small triangular cradles, or 'rests', also made of wood.

It was perfectly ordinary in its appearance.

For a second both she and the Count were reflected in it, slices of black and shimmery green jade, side by side.

Onneri spoke to the theatre, but his words were for her: 'Miss Parker, I invite you please to make an inspection of the mirror. I would like you to walk all around it and to test it as you feel appropriate. Touch it if you like, and then reassure my audience here that it is not special, or tampered with, or subject to any kind of hocus-pocus.'

Posie cast a look out into the crowd again.

She saw Richard hunched forward. He shook his head imperceptibly at her: *don't touch it.*

She saw Inspector Oats had edged closer to the stage over on the left-hand side.

I'll have to act now too, she decided.

She smiled at the crowd, bowed, and then made a small mock-tour of the mirror, peering this way and that, pretending to tap its surface. Posie walked around the back where there was genuinely nothing unusual to see.

She squatted down, looked at the legs, shook her head, pretended to tap them lightly with a white fabric-covered finger although she didn't touch a thing.

Posie joined Onneri again in the spotlight. 'I can confirm that the mirror is what it looks like,' she said clearly and as loudly as possible. 'A normal mirror.'

Onneri almost danced a jig of excitement. 'Thank you. Because I can guarantee you, one hundred per cent, that what you are all about to experience next, here at the Holborn Empire, is anything *but* normal.'

Posie moved swiftly from the stage. She hurried to her seat.

'Atta-girl,' muttered Richard as she sat down and peeled off her gloves carefully.

But Posie couldn't share Richard's obvious relief. She had a sinking, ice-like feeling in the pit of her stomach. A sense of dread, of doomed anticipation. She found herself wanting to stand up again, to shout 'STOP!' at the top of her voice. Only she wasn't quite sure what it was exactly that she wanted to stop from happening.

She moved closer to the edge of her seat, holding her breath.

Count Onneri spoke out clearly. 'There is a very old belief in my home country, to do with mirrors. They say if you call the devil, he will come to you. He will appear to you in the mirror. And that is what we will do here tonight. In this very normal mirror. I will call up the devil.'

'By Gad,' whispered Richard in an undertone, sounding annoyed. 'What bally nonsense is this?'

Screams started up in the very back of the auditorium.

There were shouts of 'Unholy trickery!' and 'Not at Christmas time!' and a small stampede as a clutch of affronted people could be heard leaving, slamming doors to the exits.

But most stayed in their places, riveted and transfixed, and the photographers had beetled out of their seats, right to the very edge of the stage, poised with their cameras and lights, ready to take the perfect picture of whatever might occur next.

There was another bow, a doff of the black hat, a flurry of the black cape, and then the magician turned and walked up close to the mirror, where his very own reflection stared back at himself.

Stared back at the whole auditorium.

He moved this way and that, as did his reflection. He took off his hat and let fly another yellow bird, as did his reflection.

A drum-roll beat up from the pit below, dulling into silence.

You could have heard a pin drop.

'Devil,' spoke Onneri. 'If you are here tonight, show yourself. Show yourself in this mirror.'

Nothing happened. Count Onneri pouted at his own reflection.

'Again. I'll try again.'

Onneri touched the glass with his wand and for a second the mirror looked as if it might fall; it rippled darkly, meltingly, and then suddenly someone in the audience screamed.

Camera flashes went off all over the place.

'IT'S THE DEVIL!' someone yelled. *Possibly Thelma from the wings?*

Everyone was immediately on their feet, and a deadly silence fell.

For in the mirror, as Onneri's reflection, stood his exact image, but with no face, just a horned sheep's skull for its head.

Onneri nodded in satisfaction, put down his wand on the floor and kicked it away. He then placed his hand on the mirror itself, as did the sheep's skull reflection, and for a moment both magician and skull-reflection were shaking hands, connected together by twin blue gloves in the mirror. *How on earth was it done?*

But then, just as suddenly as all of this horror-show had begun, Onneri pulled back his hand from the mirror, waved it around as if it were on fire, and dropped to the floor, screaming.

Posie would never forget those yells as long as she would live.

It was a shrill, unearthly sound. But was it part of this admittedly clever trick?

Everyone watched the arching, convulsing mass of black crepe robes on the stage in a dreadful, paralysed silence; it was like watching a dying insect in a spasm of agony.

'Is this meant to happen, sir?' said Sergeant Fox, standing up and whispering urgently to Richard, a seam of panic in his voice. 'It looks mighty real, sir, that's all.'

'No. I don't believe it is part of the show, Sergeant. Quick lads, up on the stage,' yelled Lovelace. 'Only don't touch a thing.'

But no-one moved.

Something was wrong here.

Very wrong.

Richard was shouting again, but not as boisterously now. 'On second thoughts, lads, don't move. Stay where you are. That's an order.'

Because in the mirror the skull-headed reflection was still standing there, unearthly, terrible, blue-gloved hand still outstretched.

A reflection of nothing, of a magician who was no longer up on his feet. The skull-headed figure suddenly moved, now clutching at his horns as if in desperation. And then it was gone.

'Is this part of the act?' yelled out a man at the back, hopefully. 'I'll give you ten points for originality, Count Onneri! Not my cup of tea though! I was expecting something Christmassy, a few angels, perhaps? Tinsel? Bells?'

'You fool!' screamed someone else, a woman, scared. 'It's the devil! It really *is* the devil! He's come for Count Onneri and now he's coming for us!'

And then there was a stampede for the exits.

It was a mad crush, a blind run of terror by the audience, most not sure if what they had seen was real or trickery. Most not wanting to stay and find out.

Posie saw the woman she had half-recognised from earlier as Genevieve Townsend pulling a scarf around her head; the actress was desperate not to be recognised amid this ruckus, beetling for an exit. To be away from anything which could tarnish her valuable reputation.

'It must be a double, or a puppet, standing in a kind of transparent box,' whispered Richard Lovelace to himself, frowning.

Posie was dismissive. 'No, darling. The mirror was thin. Normal. It was a mirror. Not a box, or cabinet. What we saw there is not possible.'

As they spoke the mirror itself tipped over, frontwards, right onto the floor in front of the prone magician, revealing itself to be a normal mirror after all.

It shattered into a hundred thousand pieces, all over the floor and over Onneri himself, and there was no box, or hidden panel behind it, no puppet or double.

Only the empty stage itself.

The journalists were all standing up, open-mouthed. They edged closer, confused.

But Richard had complete charge of the scene, and Doctor Poots and he were now heading up on stage, and Inspector Oats and Sergeant Fox were shouting at the journalists to leave.

'Get out, now!' shouted Oats to all and sundry at the top of his voice, red in the face, thoroughly enjoying himself and all the drama.

'Get out to the foyer, you blimmin' toerags. And wait there for the Chief Commissioner. For instructions. Otherwise, I'll personally see tomorrow's first editions don't run off the presses tonight, and then who'll be in trouble, eh? ALL OF YOU!'

Posie watched Dr Poots and Richard talking, squatting at the magician's side on the stage. She saw the shake of the doctor's head, the set of Richard's shoulders, the heap of black upon the floor.

Whether or not it had been the devil in the mirror, Count Onneri was dead, and it seemed he had been murdered. Murdered with his own magic mirror trick.

But why?

And how?

And by whom?

Posie hadn't liked or known the man, but he'd given her a jolly nice little introduction tonight, and she'd make good on his description of her as being a detective who solved every case she took on.

She vowed there and then to solve whatever had happened here tonight, and quickly.

Right in time for Christmas.

* * * *

PART TWO
(Murder in the Theatre)

Chapter Four

The body had been taken away.

The journalists had been sent on their way back to Fleet Street, amid frissons of excitement, and the gobsmacked crowds were dispersed through snowy streets.

Two bobbies stood sentry outside the Holborn Empire, next to the still-blazing beacons.

The theatre had become a hive of frenzied activity, overrun by Scotland Yard and with everything being directed by Lovelace.

In the foyer a huge fire in an old Victorian hearth burned merrily, and near a small, fake Christmas tree with red baubles glued onto its branches, Richard Lovelace was giving quick, careful instructions to Sergeant Fox.

Through the open doors to the theatre itself you could see the Scotland Yard Forensics team still up on stage: picking things up, dusting things down, patting walls, rattling scenery. Looking for anything. They all wore special thick rubberised suits and masks, protecting themselves from dangerous substances.

The hand-held metal mirror with the word 'MURDER' etched into it had already been confirmed by Doctor Poots as being laden with tiny crystals of strychnine, and it was presumed they would find more.

Teams of bobbies were combing the building, looking for anything unusual.

But what on earth wasn't unusual here? Posie wondered.

Inspector Rainbird, who happened to be Posie's secretary's husband, was clucking like an anxious hen, feverishly checking his notepad in the foyer, having interviewed the five-piece band, up by the stage.

He'd already interviewed the girl who had sold tickets for the show in the small box office. He had also telephoned to the Manager of the Holborn Empire, who hadn't been at the theatre for the actual show, being the Manager of over thirty such theatres, and right now Rainbird was waiting for a reply.

He harrumphed in exasperation.

'You all right, Inspector?'

'Yes, Miss Parker,' Rainbird muttered. 'But there's basically nothing to report. The girl in the office strikes me as airhead; can't remember much of what she's done all evening, apart from file her blimmin' nails! And the Manager is one of those with too much on...No-one is giving me anything useful at all. No-one seems to have known Onneri personally, and no-one saw anything strange.'

'Yes, it does sound frustrating.'

But hadn't the whole magic show been strange?

What was it they were missing here?

Rainbird hurried off again on Lovelace's orders to join Sergeant Fox in finding out more details about Olli Onneri's background, and Posie watched him limping away.

Posie had, unenthusiastically, received her own set of instructions from her husband.

In the comfort of the warm foyer with its fire and its thick cork carpet, where several cosy-looking armchairs and a scruffy-looking coffee-table had been dragged in by some of the policemen, a group had been formed on Lovelace's orders.

It was a sorry little group, and so far, it was made up only of women.

There was Posie herself, supposedly in charge, and the secretary, Miss Peterson, in her bright purple suit, and lastly, Onneri's wife, Thelma, cloaked in a black blanket.

A kind of grim terror had gripped the two young women who had worked for the magician, and they sat in a rigid silence on the armchairs: waiting, waiting.

Miss Peterson was trembling even more than before, and her unattractive green eyes were blotchy and red from crying.

Posie had stayed silent so far, not even attempting small talk, or polite conversation, and the two women employees looked relieved when Lovelace finally bounded over, pulling out paper and pen from inside his jacket pocket, introducing himself in his formal capacity as Chief Commissioner of London's Police Force.

He offered cigarettes to the women, not his own brand, but a packet of 'Players'; designed to appeal to women as much as to men.

He lit one for himself unhurriedly and shook out the match. Miss Peterson didn't take one, but sat primly waiting, whilst Thelma seemed relieved at having something to occupy herself with and she made a performance of arching her back in the chair in a sultry fashion and blowing a near-perfect smoke ring in Richard's direction. Then another.

But Posie was preoccupied: what was it she had seen which had given her the feeling that the main clue to Onneri's death was right here in this wretched theatre?

Had it been in front of her today?

And if so, what was it? And why would it be here, anyhow?

She almost missed her husband's opening gambit; the way he moved from bland pleasantries to cut-throat questioning.

'*Who* was Count Onneri?' Richard Lovelace demanded briskly, his green eyes reflecting the orange of the fire.

He looked from woman to woman, rested back in his armchair, crossed his legs casually, carried on smoking his unfamiliar cigarette patiently.

An awkward silence hung palpably in the air, along with the blue pungent smoke.

'I will ask you once again, ladies, and I would appreciate an answer this time. *Who* was Onneri? I know there is no Count of that name: we have checked the registers of births at Somerset House on the Strand, and with all the appropriate foreign embassies already, and we conclude, as indeed, most would initially suspect, it was a stage-name. A bit of pomp. So who was he?'

At the continued silence he rustled out of his inner pocket a sheet of paper and Posie recognised Fox's untidy scrawl in the dark-green ink Fox usually favoured.

Lovelace read selected pieces of the note aloud:

'Our Count Onneri is a mystery man. He pops up about a month ago in London, seemingly out of nowhere. He books the Hammersmith Apollo for January. And then he strides into the Ritz Hotel and pays for a suite there on the top floor, all in fresh bank notes of one pound each. He pays for a three-month stay there, as if that's the most normal thing in the world, right up to the end of January. Unfortunately, we can't trace those bank notes, as the Hotel Manager has cashed them and re-circulated them. Shame. But the Hotel Manager *could* tell us something useful…' Here Lovelace consulted Fox's notes again.

He looked up and smiled: '…the Hotel Manager saw Count Onneri's passport when he first arrived and it was absolutely convincing. There was no doubt in the Manager's mind that the Count was anyone other than who he said he was. But the Hotel Manager could not remember the nationality of the Count, or the country which had issued the passport, or even the colour of the cover. Worst luck. Although I'm reckoning that what we are dealing with is a set of faked papers, a fake passport, albeit of the very, very best quality.'

Miss Peterson's green eyes boggled. '*I* never had any doubts about his identity, Inspector,' she said in her low, beautifully sonorous voice. Posie saw how the secretary's thin hands and arms trembled violently, and Posie felt very sorry for the girl. She seemed an innocent, really.

'Richard,' chimed in Posie quickly, 'didn't Onneri tell us he returned from America a month ago? Perhaps it *was* his real name, and he simply added the title as a vanity? Perhaps you should get your men to check the boat logs of travellers arriving from America to England one month back?'

'It's in hand.'

Posie ploughed on: 'And Onneri must have travelled over with his friend, Matt Jenkins? The man in charge of his magical tricks? He was American, wasn't he? Where is he, anyhow? Shouldn't he be here, now? With us?'

Lovelace laughed, but it came out almost as a snarl.

'He *should* be here, yes. But it seems our friend Mr Jenkins has done a runner. It's known in my trade as a "midnight flit". Handy, eh? Which means he is our prime suspect in the murder of his boss. Most people who run do so for a reason. He seems to have left with the delightful Count Onneri's blue duffle bag, which probably contained any documents indicating the man's true identity. An all-ports alert has been put out for Jenkins. He's distinctive, at least. If he's caught trying to leave the country by any method, he will be returned to us here in London pretty quickly. And charged with murder.'

Lovelace stubbed out his cigarette on a battered coaster on the coffee-table. He fished inside his pocket again and drew out his 'Players' again.

He lit up for a second time, drew the smoke into his lungs greedily, threw his head back and unhurriedly exhaled. Posie watched the two women stare at her husband, uncertain as to his next move.

He turned to the secretary.

'And you, Miss Peterson? I understand you are a relative of the great Houdini himself? But you're not American, like him, are you? That's an English accent you have there.'

The girl nodded and her ugly pinched face was lit up earnestly, and her frog-like eyes boggled.

'That's right, Inspector. I'm a relative, but only by marriage. My mother, Bess Houdini's sister, she came over here before I was born. I've only met my uncle Harry once, sir, back in 1919, when he was doing his sell-out shows in London, but a kinder man you couldn't hope to meet. I cabled him in New York and asked him to write me a telegram of introduction to Count Onneri and I delivered it myself to the Ritz Hotel. I've always been fascinated by magic and I saw Count Onneri's advertisement for an on-stage assistant, sir, but I was too late...that role had gone. It was a shame. He offered me the position of secretary instead.'

'Ah, yes...' Richard did his best not to look surprised, and Posie herself wondered at the naivety or downright idiocy of the girl in front of her.

Had she really believed she could appear on stage?

Gracious, the stage demanded beauty, even of a very tarnished kind like Onneri had managed to find in Thelma.

Miss Peterson with her unfortunate face and nervy manner would never have even made it through an audition, let alone got a job.

Thirty seconds or so ticked by, and Thelma Onneri's cigarette was burning low.

On the pretext of collecting a normal ashtray, Posie walked over to a wall on the far side of the foyer which was covered in framed photographs, idly collecting up a filthy glass dish from the shelf there where half-empty wine glasses had been hurriedly stashed. She tipped out the ash on the shelf itself, her eyes quickly scanning the images in front of her.

And then she almost gasped aloud.

In front of her was a close-up head-shot of Houdini himself, his frizzy black hair parted into two identical wings and the intense stare making him instantly recognisable. It was signed, '*1919, Holborn Empire. The Strangest Time of all! Best Wishes, HOUDINI.*'

So Houdini *had* played here, after all.

Onneri obviously hadn't known that; he had said he had met Houdini later, in 1920, and certainly not here.

Next to the head-shot was a smaller picture of Houdini together with his wife, Bess, who was evidently a compact, neat woman with similar black hair to her husband.

The couple stood next to each other, but not really next to each other, as Bess was sealed up inside a glass tank with fish swimming around her body and Houdini was holding a large, oversized key, as if about to set her free. The inscription said '*FUN AND GAMES, 1919, Best Wishes, from the Houdinis.*'

Long-ago magical tricks, lost keys, lost meanings.

There was another picture featuring Houdini, right at its centre, but this one was more obscure, and not as cheery. The great Harry Houdini sat at its very centre, but awkwardly, among a few players who were dressed in a range of strange clothing including clown outfits, and Pierrot doll outfits.

Two of the men dressed as Pierrot dolls were big and burly, and this made them seem grotesque. Threatening. One of the Pierrot doll-men wore a black cape over the top of his costume and played with a top-hat in his huge hands.

One man dressed up as a clown was slight, with a very sad painted-on mouth, and a sad crying face and over-large pom-poms sewn on his white jacket, all in a row. He stood next to Bess Houdini, on whose other side stood a girl, dressed in identical fashion to the sad clown, only her face was painted with an exaggerated smile, and her fair gossamer-like hair was piled up in that old-fashioned

Edwardian way, like a birds-nest on top of her head. She looked slightly familiar but underneath all that thick make up she could have been anyone really.

The feeling of the group in the photograph was restless, and a nervous energy seemed to be caught up within the picture, fizzing palpably. Perhaps the group had been snapped after or before a particularly daunting trick had taken place?

Perhaps a trick had gone wrong? Or maybe they had been about to embark on a new trick?

There was no cheerful inscription here, just a gold photographer's stamp with the year '1919' embossed in a corner.

Posie took her seat again, put the ashtray down. She broke into the silence which was now awkward.

'Do either of you ladies know where Matt Jenkins, *if* that is his name, might be?'

Both women shook their heads. Posie pushed on: 'And was he a real American?'

Miss Peterson nodded, licking at her big, crowded teeth nervously, unattractively. 'I think so, yes. But he was that sort who don't say much, Miss Parker. But he was definitely American.'

'Pah!' Thelma Onneri exploded into what seemed like laughter, but could well have been chokes. 'Who are you kiddin', lovey?'

Richard hurriedly offered the blonde woman another cigarette, and took care over lighting it for her.

Thelma blew a wonky smoke ring in Miss Peterson's direction, and hunkered down inside her black blanket.

'Matthew Jenkins is no more an American than I'm a Countess, lovey. And that's not his real name, either. You've had the wool pulled right over your fetchin' little froggie green eyes, dearie.'

Thelma took another drag on her cigarette, more confident now that she had committed herself to speaking:

'Matt Jenkins is as English as I am, and an Eastender, you mark my words. He was probably born and brought up not a mile from me and me mam, somewhere along the East India Dock Road.'

So now they were getting somewhere.

'Why do you think that?' asked Lovelace, carefully, anxious not to make the confidence dry up altogether. But Posie noticed him make a quick note in his leather-covered flip-pad.

'Just the way he reacted to some of the things I said, sir. I'd use a bit of cockney slang 'ere and there and he always knew *exactly* what it meant. It was really particular, local stuff, too. It would 'ave been really obscure to *you*, sir, beggin' your pardon. Let alone to an American. It started accidentally, see? I forgot meself one evenin' and used all my old slang words, and later I realised Matt had understood me perfect like! So, then I kept on goin', and I used more and more of the slang. We was all stayin' in that suite together, you see. We ate together at night, and that's when I realised. He was an Eastender, like me.'

'Interesting.'

'I could do with a drink, guv, and I don't just mean hot tea. Is anythin' goin'?'

Lovelace turned, clicked his fingers in the direction of a bobby. 'Get us all some brandy, man, will you? From the theatre bar. Quickly, too. The ladies here are cold, and they've had a bad shock.'

'Right you are, sir.'

The brandy arrived, cheap stuff, but it came with the promise of some more truth.

Lovelace poured a generous helping for the blonde woman. She knocked it back in one gulp. He poured another unquestioningly.

'And what is your part in this, Madam? And your real name, perhaps? Because I don't think it is Thelma Onneri, is it? Although I'll not write what you tell me down, not yet. Maybe not ever.'

He closed his notebook, rested it on his knee as if he never intended to pick it up again.

The woman wiped her mouth and eyes, smeared the lipstick and panstick and red glittered eyeshadow which were applied to her face in so many careful layers.

She laughed: 'My real name's Minnie, Inspector. Minnie Wheeler. And until one month ago I was carin' for my poor dyin' mam on the same draughty road, in the same damp little hole of a house that I was born in. And then she died.'

Minnie took another swig of brandy. Lovelace poured again, right up to the brim. 'What happened then, Minnie?'

'I saw an advertisement, Inspector. That's what.'

Another swig.

'It was in a trade magazine, guv, for dancers, singers, theatre workers: *The Revue*. You know it? I was needin' a job, smartish: I had a funeral to pay for, didn't I? I needed a place to stay, too: the landlord was kickin' me out. I'm really a troupe dancer, but I'd 'ave taken anythin', to be honest with you. I was desperate. And this particular advert, it answered all my prayers.'

'Do you remember what the advert said, Minnie?'

'Nah, Inspector. But I can do better than remember. 'Ere!'

She dug inside her black blanket and got out a small crushed-velvet bag, which she opened. Two royal-blue satin gloves fell out of it, which she ignored, and she scrabbled at the bottom of the bag and pulled out a crumpled piece of paper with smudged black printing on it, a couple of inches high.

''ere you go, guv.'

Lovelace read it and passed it to Posie, who hadn't been able to avert her eyes from the blue gloves lying crumpled on the floor.

She read the typed lines.

WANTED: MAGICIAN'S ASSISTANT

1. You must be:

- free to work for me for six months, minimum.
- five feet, four inches tall and weigh no more than eight stone exactly.
- hair and eye colour is unimportant.
- able to keep any professional secrets of mine in a confidential manner. You must never gossip about what you do or see.
- I may require many things of you, and you must be open-minded.

2. In return I will:

- keep you in the utmost of style and comfort, including providing all meals and bed and board.
- pay you two pounds per week as wages.

(REPLY IF INTERESTED TO LEICESTER SQUARE: POSTBOX 39.)

Posie found the mention of weight and height objectionable, and said so.

But Minnie just shrugged.

'That's quite normal, Miss, in my line of work: dancers have to be a certain height and weight. I thought it was too good to be true, actually, and it was. But I stuck at it. Onneri's wages were crazily good. Which made up for some of the weirdness.'

'You didn't *actually* marry him, did you?' asked Posie warily.

'Nah, lovey. I'm hungry and desperate but I'm not stupid.'

'So, you had to *pretend* to be Onneri's wife?' asked Lovelace, frowning. 'Why?'

Minnie laughed. 'Dunno, really. It was one of the first things he told me I would have to do: pretend to be his wife. I think he thought it gave him more authenticity, to have a wife. Just like Houdini, see? With his wife, Bess, up on stage as a cozy double act. But old Onneri went too far with the whole "Countess" lark. Anyone could see that it didn't ring true about me. Or about us, as a couple. Onneri realised it too. He got angry at me sometimes. I suppose he wished he'd chosen a classier sort of girl, but it was too late to change: I knew all his tricks and secrets by now, didn't I?'

'He lashed out?' asked Lovelace, softly.

'Yes. Occasionally. Old Onneri had a nasty temper, see? He could be vicious. Especially when things didn't go as he wanted, which was often, and sometimes he'd fly off the handle with no warnin'. He'd strike me with that wand across the face. I think he put the old white stuff up his nose every day too, and that didn't improve his mood; not one bit. He's been all right these last two days though, since Miss Peterson came in all excited-like with the news we had this theatre for free! What a blessin' that was! He was almost hummin' with joy about it. Hoppin' around, he was! And he didn't have time to hit me, either. We were practicin' so hard, see? I kept tellin' meself there wasn't much longer to go, and I had the pound notes already saved up. It was my nest egg.'

Lovelace looked suddenly hopeful. 'Do you have the notes, Minnie? Can my Forensics boys examine them over night? You'll have them right back again tomorrow.'

The girl nodded. 'They're back at the Ritz. Under my mattress in my little room. I take it me and Miss Peterson can still sleep there tonight?'

'Certainly.'

'Good. I ain't got nowhere else to go yet.'

Minnie Wheeler stood, yawned, the brandy slowing her down. 'I think I'd like to go there now. I feel so tired. The Count was an 'orrible man, but he didn't deserve that death today: no way. It looked blimmin' excrutiatin'.'

Minnie gathered the blanket about her, letting it slip slightly. Rather than one of the brightly-coloured tulle dresses she'd worn up on stage, Posie saw she was wearing a white man's shirt with a black dickie bow tie, and a black tuxedo jacket and trousers.

Suddenly it all made sense.

The blue gloves fallen to the floor made sense. The man's suit. The exact specification of an assistant's desired weight and height made sense. The high wages and the need for secrecy.

The black blanket wrapped about Minnie was not a blanket at all: it was actually a cape.

There was only one practical thing missing.

A sheep's skull.

'*You!*' Posie breathed, standing up.

'*You're* the devil in the mirror!'

****

Chapter Five

The woman crumpled then, and admitted it.

Minnie *was* the devil in the mirror, and she tried her best to draw on the back of the coaster how the ingenious trick worked.

While Onneri stood in front of a completely normal mirror on the stage below, with his back to the audience, *she* stood on a platform directly above him. Right above him.

The platform was hidden by the top of the curtains.

She faced the stage on her high-up platform, wearing an identical suit to the magician himself, but with a horned skull strapped over her head.

Minnie stood in front of an identical mirror to the one on stage below, but it was positioned at a very particular angle, with its top part nearer her head than the bottom part, and it was held like that by special transparent cords.

Bright flash-lights surrounded her to illuminate the scene.

And in the space in front of her, right under her mirror, cut into the platform, was a large square dangerous hole.

At a given agreed moment Onneri's mirror below was also pulled by transparent strings so that it, too, moved backwards into the identical slanted angle to Minnie's mirror above, but imperceptibly to the audience members.

The two mirrors were both now lined up directly in line with each other, at the same angles, ready to receive each other's reflections.

And as soon as the 'slanting' of Onneri's mirror was done, Onneri and Minnie began to coordinate their moves, in tandem. Onneri would reach out to touch the mirror, so would Minnie. He would step back in disbelief, so would she.

'I dunno how he did it,' said Minnie. 'It was right proper magic. Apparently, I appeared in the mirror down on the stage, just as I was, in front of him. With that stinky sheep's mask on. I could also see him, up on the platform with me, in my mirror! It was creepy, clever. And that's what he wanted to keep a secret!'

Minnie exhaled in disbelief. 'It was blimmin' dangerous work though. He told me if I lost concentration and fell down the hole which had been cut in front of me up on that platform, I'd be dead on the floorboards below, and if I didn't break my neck fallin', he'd break it for me as I'd have ruined his best ever trick.'

'What a truly lovely fella,' said Lovelace. But he was staring at the coaster with a look of genuine admiration.

'I'll show this to the Forensics team; perhaps it may help them understand what was going on, or how Onneri died. It's ingenious, though, I'll give him that. He perhaps was a true genius? A rival for the best of magicians. It's so simple, yet so clever: like a child's giant periscope. Designed for the stage!'

Posie watched as Minnie Wheeler and Miss Peterson were led off to a taxi outside by a bobby, both obviously keen to get back to the luxury of the Ritz, not knowing how long the arrangement would last, and she watched their retreating backs disappear into the swirling snow.

Something still niggled at Posie, but she didn't know quite what it was.

Sergeant Fox had entered the foyer, clutching at a battered leather document folder, and Posie watched as Richard gave him orders. She came close as Fox scribbled them down in a small pad.

'Get to the Ritz right away, Sergeant. Get the girl, Minnie Wheeler, to show you where her pound notes are hidden and then take them along to the Bank of England. I don't care that it's late, or the week before Christmas. Hopefully we can get a trace on the notes and work out their origin. We'll work out *where* Onneri was sourcing his money from and then at last we'll get something on this wretched dead fella, eh?'

'Right you are, sir.'

Richard glanced at his wristwatch. It was now almost nine o'clock. 'Any news of big burly Matthew Jenkins, the supposedly American lad? *If* that's his name, which I doubt. Any news from the ports, train stations, airports?'

Fox's long, bloodhound-like face looked doleful. 'No. Afraid not, sir. I'll keep you informed.'

'A slight change of plan, Fox. Extend the search, lad. Get local policemen to check every watering-hole and place of refuge along the East India Dock Road.'

'Here, sir? In London?'

'Yep. He might be intending to go to ground there. I've received new information that Matt Jenkins might be from that area: I don't yet know if this is accurate information but we have a duty to investigate. In my experience men frequently go back to the place of their birth, their comfort zone, when they are in trouble. Often desperate men are found quickly, and Jenkins must be bally well desperate.'

'Noted, sir. You really think he's our murderer, sir?'

Lovelace narrowed his eyes. 'He's our number one suspect, for sure. Seems likely he's done a flit with Onneri's money, and papers, and drugs, and perhaps his book of professional tricks. Maybe they had a professional disagreement? About who was really the brains behind the whole piece, eh? The poison on those mirrors strikes me as an odd note, though, as do the actual messages themselves. Not quite a man's thing to do, is it?'

'No, sir,' replied Fox demurely.

'It doesn't seem like a man's crime: poison rarely is. But we don't know exactly how Onneri died yet, do we, sir? Maybe that stuff with the poisoned mirrors was no more than a load of window-dressing. We still don't yet know if poison was the actual cause of death, do we? Or if that in itself was just a red herring, sir?'

Silence.

Poison.

Murder.

Mirrors.

Posie chewed her lip. Thinking. Replaying what she had seen occur on the stage earlier: the tricks, the assistants, the mirror, the music, the booming American voice.

She felt like laughing. She'd checked the mirror when she was called up on stage, but it had never occurred to her to look *up*.

If she had she would have seen Minnie in her strange outfit positioned directly above her head, teetering on the edge of a lethal trap door.

Fox seemed anxious to leave: 'Is there anything else I can do now, sir?'

'You should contact Sam Stubbs, Sergeant,' Posie cut in. 'He'll be at the *Associated Press* offices right now, editing like crazy for tomorrow's edition. He was sitting on the second row here tonight with his photographer. I'm sure he'd have taken a decent snap of the pair of them, Onneri and Matt Jenkins, together, when Jenkins came on to help him with the heavy chain trick, or when he handed him the knives from the wings. You could get several copies developed and circulate the photograph around a bit, couldn't you? Certainly, in the East End, and at the London docks?'

Richard nodded. 'Mnnn, good point, darling.' He lit up another cigarette, but this time from his own battered pack of Turkish gaspers. He started to smoke, but not with much enjoyment.

He was lost in his own chain of thought, and he started speaking it aloud, Posie and Sergeant Fox trying to keep up as he rambled.

'Something strikes me as off here. How come Onneri was so bally rich? He stays at the Ritz. Like a film star. In a *suite*! He's throwing pound notes about to assistants, all over the place! It doesn't add up. Not even Houdini himself would have done that. And what's the history of this fella? Was Onneri *really* in America? Was Onneri doing the same sort of magic shows over there? This clever magic mirror trick? Was Onneri well-known there? Fox, do some digging. Start with New York: that's where Houdini is based, I'm sure of it. You could try and get an American journalist onto it, perhaps: someone who specialises in entertainment? If you're speaking to Sam Stubbs anyway, you could ask if he knows of anyone suitable over there?'

'That all sounds like a big job, sir.' Fox sounded like he was biting down his annoyance.

'The night is long, Sergeant. Get Smallbone onto it, if you don't have time: he likes a good chase. This is a murder case, Fox, and thanks to our murder victim being a publicity-seeking lunatic, Count Onneri's death and his show will be all over the front pages of every newspaper in the country tomorrow. Not to mention the clamouring hoards who will want their ticket-monies paid back to them for the cancelled Apollo shows in January! What a mess it will all be. We need to solve this, and hopefully within the next day or so. The reputation of the Police Force is at stake. All of our reputations. On such a high-profile case as this, Fox, there are advantages for us all. Rewards, *promotions...*'

It was a well-known fact that the very capable but still

quite young Sergeant Fox had been after an Inspectorship for ages. This was an easy bait for Richard to hand out. And Posie sensed a quickness in the Sergeant's manner which hadn't been there a moment before.

He stood up just a little straighter.

'Anything else, sir?'

Richard paused, taking a final drag of his smoke before grinding it underfoot on the coconut-rush matting of the entrance hall floor. 'Yes, I think I've changed my mind about something, about *someone*. When you've got the pound notes off her, I want you to bally well arrest Minnie Wheeler at the Ritz.'

Posie gasped.

She clutched her husband's arm. 'WHAT? What on earth, Richard? The girl took you into her confidence! Gave you the East End lead for Jenkins!'

'*If* that's accurate, darling.'

'Even so. What motive do you think she would have? She was completely honest with you here.'

Richard looked annoyed. 'How do we know she was honest? And as to motive…'

He tapped his index finger dramatically to illustrate his point. 'She's got nothing, and she's desperate: she said as much herself. And she'd had the good fortune to meet a man with a lot of ready money. Perhaps she got a taste for it and wanted more? Onneri said no, and she killed him…'

He tapped his middle finger. 'Second, she's resourceful and canny, and she knew and understood the magic tricks Onneri was operating.'

Posie shook her head. 'You're wrong, my love. I don't think Minnie did understand. Certainly not the way the periscope mirror trick actually worked. She didn't get it. Minnie was frightened of it.'

Lovelace shrugged. 'Let's assume she *did* understand. Perhaps Minnie Wheeler felt the stuff in the advertisement about keeping secrets didn't apply to her? Or perhaps she was trying to blackmail Onneri for more money? For a lump sum in order to keep the magic tricks confidential? He refused to play ball, and so she killed him, eh?'

He tapped his ring finger. 'My third and final point is my strongest. We know Onneri was beating her. Perhaps Minnie had had enough? The mirrors sent to him could be something about appearances, couldn't they? A sort of dramatic warning to stop him from beating her? It would have been easy enough to make it look as if the shards of mirrors were 'sent' to the Ritz, where she was also staying, and easy enough for her to have the hand-mirror sitting here ready for Onneri today in an old cake-box. Minnie was in all the same places as Onneri, all of the time. It would have been child's play to get the mirrors to him, and child's play to source the poison in the first place: a clever girl like that from the East End...'

Lovelace turned to Fox, nodded grimly. 'Yes: I think I have in mind Minnie Wheeler as our prime suspect now, Sergeant. I don't think I'd put the poisoned mirrors past her. She's a survivor, that one. Arrest her and make it known we have made the arrest. Put her in the cells at the Yard, and perhaps by morning, when she's been away from the glamour of the Ritz a little bit, she'll feel like talking again.'

'At once, sir. And I'll carry on pursuing Matt Jenkins?'

'Yes. Absolutely. One or the other of them are responsible for this, mark my words.'

Posie's face was red, bursting, outrage swelling within her and she wanted to scream at the injustice here. She didn't know Minnie Wheeler, not one bit, but she had sensed an earthiness, a truth, to the girl.

Because who in life liked to declare they were desperate?

Perhaps there was an element of sympathy at play here, too. The bruises under the thick make-up had pierced through to Posie's heart, and besides, Posie had a soft spot for a cockney.

Her best friend, Dolly, who had recently vanished in mysterious circumstances, was also from the East End of London: a girl who had similarly struggled, alone, to make her own way in a world of men who laid down the rules.

Posie watched as Fox turned to leave, and was about to open her mouth and let rip a flurry of anger, when an excitable Inspector Rainbird came limping in and collided with his younger colleague. He looked put out for a second, dusting off thick snowflakes from his putty-coloured coat sleeve, but he cheered up when he saw Lovelace right in front of him.

He dragged a violet form from his inside pocket, waved it triumphantly.

'I have the cause of death, sir. The preliminary report from Doctor Poots! He finished it in record time; got Count Onneri's body taken to the police morgue just up the road here in Camden. Saved time that way.'

'Go on, man,' growled Lovelace, who was in the process of shrugging on his own overcoat.

'Electrocution!'

Lovelace, and Posie, and Fox, right over at the door, all froze.

Stunned.

Rainbird, enjoying his moment of drama, read snippets aloud. 'The doctor says the murder victim suffered a massive cardiac arrest as a result of a ginormous electric shock. The shock was so large that the fingertips and satin of the gloves were simply burned away. There are other classic signs, too: scorch marks and all hair on the body standing on end. The shock would have been enough to kill anyone, Poots says here.'

Rainbird waved the form. 'Our man was a habitual drug addict, apparently, and he had a dreadfully infected cut on his right hand; recent, it looked like. And there were high levels of strychnine poisoning in his blood. Poots says he would have died from the strychnine within another twenty-four hours, even without the electric shock which finished him off.'

Lovelace was grim. He looked over at Posie and the green sparkly light in his eyes seemed to have faded right away.

'Thank God you didn't touch that mirror, darling. It must have been wired up somehow, so that when Onneri touched it, the whole thing was alive with voltage, and it killed him. I'd better go and get the Forensics boys to pull it apart up there on stage, if they haven't yet done so.'

'Sir?' Rainbird was stabbing at the bottom of the violet form. 'Poots says he has to bring something else to your attention. An important point. The dead man's hands were very distinctive, sir.'

'Oh?'

'They were covered in a terrible burn, sir. Like acid had been thrown all over them, he says. Healed, years ago, but still very distinctive.'

Lovelace looked thoughtful. 'The blue gloves were not just for show, then, eh? Mnnn. But why does that sound familiar?'

He frowned. 'No, it escapes me...Anything else, Rainbird?'

'That's it from the good doctor, sir,' said Rainbird, clearly pleased with himself. 'But I *do* have news from Mr Gulliver, the Managing Director of this theatre. He just called back. Apparently, he was contacted three weeks ago. He was asked if the theatre could be hired for one night only, the 18th December, for a show for Count Onneri. It suited Gulliver well as he has a new variety show for Christmas starting up next week, so the theatre was empty anyway. There was no request for a full staff, just the one ticket office girl who apparently makes herself quite handy, and the five-piece in-house band.'

'How was Gulliver contacted?' demanded Lovelace. 'And how was he paid? More pound notes, I expect?'

'No, sir. Gulliver's fee was met, in advance, by cheque. In the name of a chap called "Dean", he believes. Twenty pounds. It cleared three weeks ago without any problems.'

Posie frowned. 'Dean? Could that be Onneri's real name? Although he told me that the show at the Holborn Empire had been an unexpected last-minute opportunity, an unplanned thing. He told me it had been gifted to him for free.'

'He *said* many things, darling.'

Posie didn't like the way her husband was making her sound like a silly girl, eager to believe just about everything she heard. And in front of the policemen, too.

'I suppose Kettner's is off now, is it?' she said icily.

She rather hoped it was. Her stomach was like a turgid ashy blob in her insides, and she had things she needed to attend to.

'That's right, Posie love. I'll see you back at the flat later tonight.'

'You might.' But this part she mumbled, and as she watched her husband and Rainbird loop back into the theatre to prod at deadly electrics, and as Sergeant Fox ambled off into the snowy night, she resolved she'd get to the bottom of things now.

Posie didn't know why, but she knew she had to go back exactly the way she had come.

She needed to go downstairs again, back into the awful dressing-room from earlier.

* * * *

Chapter Six

Smiling at the bobby positioned by the small closed box office, Posie hurried off through the foyer, past the smiling pictures of Houdini, and into the back of the auditorium.

Ignoring the many men up on stage in white coats, she pulled aside the black gauzy curtain and headed down the partly-concealed staircase she and Richard had used only two hours earlier, although it seemed as if it had been years ago now, and she was relieved to find that downstairs in the basement everything was lit up brightly, with electric bulbs turned on everywhere.

Perhaps the Forensics team were down here too, or else the lower floor had been forgotten about in all the chaos and pandemonium?

Reaching the bottom, she turned right, retracing her earlier steps along the winding passageway. Ahead of her were the dressing-rooms, the first one, which Onneri had been using, still had lights on inside, with the door wide open.

Outside in the corridor was the mad pre-show detritus of the team which no-one had yet had a chance to clear up: red cream glitter on the floor in globules; rainbow tulle skirts all in a tangle; an upturned packet of powdered rosin; a white dove, dead on the floor.

A frightened tiny golden bird was flying backwards and forwards along the corridor, tweeting pathetically. Trapped.

'Golly gosh,' muttered Posie, stepping over all of the mess.

The dressing-room was as she had last seen it. Grotty, grimy, all except for the area Onneri had occupied. The hand-mirror and the small fragments of mirror with their grotesque – and chillingly accurate – messages, had all vanished. Probably Forensics had got down here first.

Posie marched over to the Count's chair and sat in it wearily. She looked ahead at herself in the mirror with its bright pearly round bulbs set all around it, fancy as a necklace.

'What were you doing here, Mister?' she whispered.

'Why were you here, tonight, Count Onneri? And why did you have to die here tonight? What had you *done*? Because I saw your face, and you were scared. Your eyes were scared, and that had nothing to do with how much cocaine you may or may not have taken…'

She stared hard into the mirror, at her own face which she knew so well, at the blue eyes which looked a little tired beneath their black kohl and thick lashings of Maybelline mascara. The spidery lines which she concealed very well with powder.

She sighed, careful not to touch anything on the vanity table itself where the strychnine-loaded fragments had rested.

'Of course, this is all a stupid idea,' Posie whispered aloud at her reflection. 'But I couldn't shake off the feeling that something happened here. Because Olli Onneri certainly knew this place, this room. I saw his face in the mirror. I'm convinced of it.'

In years to come Posie would wonder why she hadn't been more scared at what happened next.

Why she hadn't screamed aloud.

Because all of a sudden the overhead light fizzled, and

went out. And then the bulbs around the mirror crackled and lost power, one by one.

The light in the corridor outside also went out, and a complete darkness seemed to reign. The tiny bird outside started tweeting desperately.

Posie sat stock-still in the chair, heart hammering inside her chest.

Breathe, breathe. I can move. I can run if I want to.

Richard is upstairs with a lot of big strong men, and I am safe.

I am safe!

But what she was telling herself went against everything she was feeling, and Posie remained rooted to the spot, as if frozen in place on the chair. A terrible prickly sensation twitched across her neck and her back, the sort of thing she normally only felt when someone was behind her, or when she was being watched.

Who is there?

She wanted to call out, to scream it, but the words never came.

Instead, there was a sudden icy breeze, as if someone had opened a window quickly, and a bang, and another bang, nearer, in the room itself, where there were no windows, and then, just as suddenly as the lights had gone out, they all came back on again.

Pop-pop-pop-pop.

Posie breathed slowly, shallowly, as she had done when she had been in labour with her only son, Kit. But at least then she had known what she was dealing with.

In the mirror she saw the odd wooden cabinet behind her, and saw that the door with all the locks attached to it was swinging in the breeze. Banging.

That had been the banging noise.

That was all.

Someone must have opened a window somewhere or, more likely, the Stage Door had been opened, and the draught had caused the doors to bang, perhaps even made a fuse trip? There was a perfectly reasonable explanation for it all.

In a giddy spasm of relief, Posie rose, went to the cupboard on the wall, intending to close the door properly.

But as she reached out, a slip of paper from inside the cupboard blew from its shelf, falling through the air, twisted, curling, ancient.

She had seen it before. Noted it in the back of her subconsciousness. She picked it up from the mildewy floor, which was sticky with stains, and Posie turned it this way and that in the dressing-room light.

Posie recognised it instantly. She'd seen a copy of it not an hour before, upstairs, in the foyer. On the wall. This was the same strange picture of Houdini, grouped around with people in bizarre outfits: clowns, Pierrots.

There was no date on the front of this picture and it was in bad condition. Its edges were brown and slightly green. A flush of mould and possibly a tarry brown substance covered the bottom left-hand corner.

She turned it over, and saw scratchy, tiny writing, in sharp-nibbed pencil. Bringing it right up to her line of vision, she tried to read. There were names listed there:

HOUDINI. H

DI MAGGIO. R

DEAN. E

COLLINS. J

BELL. C

HOUDINI. B

HUNTER. G

The names obviously didn't correspond with the exact location of the people in the picture, worst luck, and her excitement at seeing the name 'Dean. E,' as being the man who had paid with a cheque for tonight's show at the Holborn Empire was short-lived.

He could have been any of these people, save for the Houdini's themselves, and the smiling girl clown.

'Oh, well…'

Posie opened her small evening clutch, wishing she had her big, trusty, worn carpet bag with her tonight instead, and she placed the photograph inside it for safekeeping.

She had a tiny mauve notebook with her, with a slip of an amethyst-coloured pencil attached to it with a pink string. It was something Phyllis played with when they went on long journeys, and Posie copied down the inscription on the wall into its tiny pages: the long-ago warning from Ricky Di Maggio about not touching the cupboard.

'I've seen enough now,' she whispered to herself.

She turned to leave, promising herself she would never, ever be back, when she saw she was being watched from the open doorway.

A black shadow took up the whole space there.

Posie stiffened.

But then the shadow moved, and Posie realised a man in his late thirties, very smartly-dressed, was standing there. He was fair, handsome, with curly hair and a pink and white complexion.

'Forgive me.' He smiled, slightly embarrassed, stepping politely back out into the corridor. 'I came to find out what was happening down here; I think the electricity gave out for a minute. A faulty fuse, I expect. I didn't know anyone was actually along here, though. Are you all right, Miss?'

'Quite all right, thank you. My name is Posie Parker.'

'Ah, the famous detective? I am one of Charles Gulliver's assistants, George Loxley, and I help him run this theatre.

Mr Gulliver received a telephone call tonight about this dreadful business with Count Onneri, and he sent me over to check on things. Are you working with New Scotland Yard?'

'Ye-es.'

'I see. Then that is why you are down here; I did wonder when I saw you looking about just now, in that room.'

He means snooping, Posie supposed.

They stood together in the corridor next to the dead dove. On the floor ahead of them the golden bird had landed. It looked like its neck was broken.

Mr Loxley snapped off the lights in Onneri's dressing-room, and pulled the door to. He indicated to the other dressing-rooms down the corridor.

'It's odd, Miss Parker, as I told your Forensics people. I'm not sure why Count Onneri was using this particular dressing-room tonight, or why the others were marked as being 'OUT OF USE'. The others are far more comfortable. They've all been newly appointed; freshly painted and are right up to date with all the modern facilities. *This* room is always left closed. Nobody uses it. It's become a junk room.'

'Why, sir?'

Mr Loxley shrugged, amused. 'Actors are funny creatures, Miss Parker. Superstitious. People are wary of this particular room. There was an incident in it, once, about five years ago: someone was hurt quite badly, I think. But I wasn't here at the time, so I can't tell you more, I'm afraid.'

They walked along the corridor together. 'We should get that dressing-room made good again. We should focus on the glamour it has seen. You know Harry Houdini had a show here, and that room was used by his entourage? Well, yes, you've seen their scribblings on the wall. I saw you taking note of it all!'

Loxley winked at her. 'Theatres are certainly interesting

places, Miss Parker, and I should know. They've got it all: glamour, hope, fear, disappointment. Ghosts, too, so some would lead you to believe. We apparently have our very own lady in white.'

'Oh? That sounds very gothic!'

'She's always used as an excuse for the lights going on and off.' Mr Loxley grinned. 'I'd always plump on the side of faulty electrics as an explanation, myself.'

'Mnnn. It would seem a cosier explanation, yes.'

Upstairs, Posie watched as Mr Loxley chatted easily with the policemen and the last of the Forensics team.

She checked her small red wristwatch. It was almost ten o'clock now.

She hurriedly bundled herself into her opera coat and dashed out, out of the foyer and its warmth into a world which had become a swirling, whirling snow-scene straight from a children's picture book.

The extreme cold had forced the groups of poor real-life children to disperse, goodness only knew where, probably to Lincoln's Inn Fields, right behind them, where braziers or open bonfires sometimes burned on very cold nights in the centre of the park itself, where traditionally the poor of London sought shelter and a cup of soup.

The icy wind whistled through Posie's thin coat and she drew the collar well up, pulled her black felt hat down over her ears, and felt the snowflakes landing on her eyelashes.

The walk to her office was only ten minutes from here, and she risked it, skidding on the icy pavement, watching men ahead shovelling the snow off the walkway, and a carthorse walking slowly alongside in the road, lit up with orange lanterns for safety, laden with bags of salt on his panniers.

A horrible dense cloud of icy mist and snowy, soot-laden grey-green grubby fog was lowering itself downwards, as sometimes happened in London on the coldest of days, and Posie walked faster to be out of it quicker.

The bells of various churches were ringing out through the misty night air.

Snow muffled the bells and added a strange distortion to the peals. Ten o'clock, and the bells of St Clement Danes with its familiar 'Oranges and Lemons' peal seemed closer somehow than the bells from St Anselm's which was but a stone's throw away.

'Nearly there,' she promised herself.

She tried not to think of Minnie Wheeler, probably being separated from her hard-earned money right now and trading a cosy feather-filled hotel bed for the hard bare planks of the bleach-stinking cells in Victoria, under pain of arrest.

She tried not to think of Count Onneri himself, his cold body in the Camden morgue, his heart stopped forever, his blood inert and poisoned in his icy veins, his black-painted hair crisped and fried by electricity and covered by a white shroud.

Or of big, brawny Matt Jenkins, on the run, desperately seeking a place of safety in this relentless snow.

What on earth linked all of this?

She was heading for her office, and not home, because she needed to puzzle this out. While the children would be tucked in and sleeping by now, with Masha the Russian nanny looking after them all, Posie always felt that as soon as she entered the top-floor flat on Bury Place she was immediately 'on duty'.

Work dropped back and became unimportant. Even to herself.

It was vital she remained clear-headed, able to work with absolute dedication and clarity.

She remembered the iciness of the Grape Street office earlier, and she stopped at a small stall on the corner of High Holborn and Shaftesbury Avenue where decent bacon rolls and cups of very sugary tea were served into the small hours of each morning.

She queued among hardy revellers for a bacon roll, and on the spur of the moment bought two, and she dashed, shivering and snowflake-covered to her office.

But as she reached the top-floor landing, where only this afternoon Count Olli Onneri had stood, inviting her to his show, she saw lights were on inside the office itself, and she could see the orange glow of a roaring fire in the grate, through the glass door.

'Oh, Len!' she exclaimed under her breath. 'Thank goodness. A friendly face at last.'

And armed with the hot bacon rolls, she entered the office.

But Len was sprawled out, before the fire of the waiting room, in a sleeping bag, fast asleep. It looked like he was established there for the night.

'I'll have both rolls myself, then.' And Posie stepped carefully around him, shut the door to her own little office and lit the fire in her own grate.

She sat down at her desk, took a big sheet of blotting paper from a drawer and placed it in front of herself.

She retrieved the photograph which had fallen from the stained dressing-room cupboard, and stuck it with a tiny piece of tape at the centre, but not before writing the names inscribed on its back in big clear capitals on the side of the blotting paper.

She also wrote down Ricky Di Maggio's message from the wall.

'PROPERTY OF RICKY DI MAGGIO – DON'T TOUCH OR HOUDINI OR I WILL DARN WELL PUT A SPELL ON YOU! OR WORSE!'

Then Posie wrote a date, 1919, as the title at the top of her paper.

She'd seen the date on the identical photograph in the foyer, and hoped to goodness it was right.

But she thought it *was* correct: the other photographs Houdini had signed for the wall there had also featured the same date.

She sat back, ate the two nearly-cold rolls, marched around a bit and eventually got out her *Encyclopaedia Britannica*, which had a handy envelope for maps and enclosures at the back.

Pulling out the one marked ‘Standard Time Zone Chart of the World’, she ran a greasy, buttery finger over the coloured columns of endless time spanning the North Atlantic Ocean, and she picked up her telephone receiver accordingly.

* * * *

Chapter Seven

Posie needed help, and frankly, she didn't care if she looked an idiot in asking for it.

She decided to start at the very top.

New York was five hours behind, which meant it was about five o'clock in the afternoon there.

She asked the International Operator for her call to be placed with the Commissioner of the New York Police Department, Richard's equivalent American counterpart.

Posie knew the Commissioner was called Enright, as she'd heard Richard talking about him sometimes. He was rather famous, in fact.

As she waited on the rustling, whizzy, far-away line, she wondered what she would say to this famous American policeman, if he deigned to speak to her at all. She'd have to blag a bit.

A clipped American girl's voice was suddenly in her ear: 'You're through. Now, who did you say you were, exactly, Miss? New Scotland Yard? But this isn't a recognised line, is it?'

'I'm special branch, calling on behalf of the English Chief Commissioner, Richard Lovelace. I need to speak to Commissioner Enright, straightaway.'

'I see. Hold the line, then, would ya?'

More fizzy noise. Then a deep, gruff voice answered. 'Enright here, who's that, you say? Richard Lovelace? Of the Yard? How can I help ya, Dickie?'

Posie dropped the pretence at once. She felt too frightened of the consequences of her fraud. Maybe she was actually doing something illegal in pursuing this pretence?

'Er, well. Hullo, sir. It's not actually Dickie Lovelace, sir. It's his wife, Posie. I know your name from my husband. I hope you don't mind my calling, but I need your help, sir.'

'Say, sure. If I can. Dickie's all right? Not kidnapped or anything awful? In trouble?'

'No, he's right as rain. I'm investigating something for myself. Something American.'

A stunned silence followed. Then a tight laugh. 'Well, that sure is swell. How can I help you, Mrs Lovelace?'

'It's easy and it's hard at the same time, sir. I need to speak to the magician, Harry Houdini. I think he lives in New York and I need to get a message to him. I have a couple of questions only he can answer.'

A rip-roaring laugh met this request, and Posie suddenly felt ridiculous.

Enright spoke again after his burst of merry laughter. 'Houdini? Well, they do say that Houdini is known to be very private, and very family-oriented, and I would imagine he's hunkering down right now for the holiday season with his nearest and dearest. I could arrange for a telegram to be sent his way, if you think it might help?'

'Thank you. Well, here is the message anyhow.'

And she gave it, and felt immediately better for doing so.

'Is there anything else I can help you with, Mrs Lovelace? Anyone else over this side of the pond you'd like to chat with?'

Posie ignored his slightly patronising tone, and carried on anyway. 'Well, since you ask…'

In for a penny, in for a pound.

'Is the name Count Olli Onneri known to you, sir?'

'It is not.'

'Fine. Can you tell me if any of these names I am about to read aloud are familiar to you, sir, for any reason at all?'

'You go ahead.'

And Posie read aloud the list of names on the back of the curled-up photograph, omitting only the Houdinis themselves.

She pictured Mr Enright in his office, far, far away across the ocean.

She imagined him, big and capable, behind a huge desk in an office in a skyscraper such as she had seen in that postcard taped up in the dressing-room earlier.

Posie imagined that if he stood up he could see sparkling Christmas trees like multi-coloured necklaces for as far as the eye could see, strung out right across Central Park, and all the way along the Hudson River, and up and down the straight, sharp avenues of Manhattan with their fascinating shops and beautiful women who waited in large, empty apartments, living on a diet of hopeful glamour and the sort of happiness which comes parcelled up in glossy shopping bags.

'Nope! I can't help you, Mrs Lovelace.'

She imagined Commissioner Enright shaking his head while he stood there.

'I can't say I know any of those names, no. Sorry to disappoint you. Oh, but wait, did you say *Di Maggio*? Ricky Di Maggio? Hang on a minute.'

More rustling, what seemed like shouting in the far distance.

The Commissioner was back on the line.

'Say, ain't you lucky, Mrs Lovelace? By chance, I have our so-called Italian specialist with me today, Michael Fiaschetti; he used to run our Italian Squad here in New York, and then it all got a little too dangerous. But he knows every single Italian in this city, and he knows the Di Maggio family. This Ricky fella is something in the theatre, isn't he? Michael says Ricky is a good boy; he might be famous one day in his own right. He's gonna make sure Ricky telephones you this evening. What's your exchange there in London? Holborn 2897? Right: I've got it. Give my regards to Dickie, huh? Good speaking to you, Mrs Lovelace.'

Buzzing from this very slight triumph, Posie called Sam Stubbs over on Fleet Street.

'Wotcha, Posie. What a blimmin' night, eh? You got something for me? Or can *I* help you?'

But Sam sounded tired out, frazzled. It was half-past ten now but the night was still young for him.

'I hope so. Tell me, do you recognise any of these names?'

And she read out the list again, pausing specially over the '*Dean. E*', waiting for some spark of recognition.

Sam had a very good recall of names, faces, histories, stories. He'd done well, rising through the ranks from jobbing journalist to editor of a major national newspaper, and he was still one of the best in the job for details.

But all she got now was a sigh.

'Nah, nothing for me there, Posie. But listen up: I'm putting *you* on the front page tomorrow, you and Onneri together. A real beauty of a snap, it is. You'll want it framed. You look like Louise Brooks. Gorgeous.'

'I doubt it. Well, so long.'

She replaced the telephone receiver in its cradle and sat with her head in her hands. It was at times like this she missed the company of the old office cat, Mr Minks, a Siamese who had simply upped and left one day, walking out of their lives forever.

He would have settled here now, in front of the fire, or jumped into her lap, kept her warm. Stopped her feeling so alone.

'Penny for your thoughts, Po?'

She looked up.

It was Len.

Ruffled, rumpled, gorgeous-but-with-looks-just-turning Len. He'd pushed open the door and she hadn't heard him.

'Len! You're back early from Eastbourne. Or are you on a job tonight?'

'Nah. But I need to do some Christmas shoppin' first thing tomorrow; get a tree and all that. Thought I'd get it all done in Covent Garden, and save meself the double journey.'

'Fair enough.'

But Len looked shifty somehow: like he wasn't telling the whole truth.

Perhaps he had had a row with his wife, Aggie? It wouldn't have been the first time. And these rows seemed to be getting more and more frequent. But Posie didn't like to pry further.

'You look shattered, Po. What's 'appened? And who were all those people's names you were readin' out just now on the telephone?'

And so Posie told him about Onneri, and what had happened at the Holborn Empire. And what she had found in the dressing-room, and what didn't make sense.

Which was most of it.

She told him about all the holes; the lack of answers.

About how Onneri had no history, and could not be traced.

About the woman, Minnie, who had probably been wrongly accused of murder; about the man, Jenkins, who was running for his life.

Len threw himself into the chair opposite Posie at the desk, and he sat stretched out, head cradled in the support of his strong, perfect, overlapping hands with their clean, clipped white fingernails.

Hands.

Posie's thoughts turned to blue gloves; to a statement piece of clothing used as a way of disguising a problem.

Acid burns.

Acid...

She must have muttered this half-aloud, because suddenly Len was looking excited, on the edge of his seat.

'Acid burns? Are you *sure*? You said that your magician, Onneri, had acid burns! Oh, *now* I can help you!'

Len was almost frothing at the mouth in excitement. 'Has he only been around for about a month or two? No trace of him beforehand?'

Posie sat up straight, almost giddy with impatience. 'That's absolutely right! Why?'

Len laughed and started to roll a cigarette on his knee.

'If I'm correct, and I think I am, as the timing fits, your Count Onneri is a career criminal who has been in prison a good long while.'

'Is he? I mean – *was* he?'

Len nodded, excited: 'He was a famously brilliant safe-cracker.'

Posie gasped. 'That would make a kind of sense. But *who* was he?'

Len lit his cigarette. 'Dunno his real name. He was nicknamed "Snakes" Hunter. Mainly because he 'ad these magic fingers which were like snakes: folk said he could crack open any safe, pick any lock in the land. It was like magic. Wasn't there a "Hunter" there on your list?'

Posie checked the paper and nodded. 'Yes. A "G. Hunter."'

'Yes, thought so. Well, if it's who I think it is, he was a funny little chap: slight, delicate, good-looking in a warped way, but with these acid-damaged hands. Said he'd had an accident with a big bank safe. He wore the scars like a badge of honour. He was a criminal who couldn't be caught, and he had a wingman. A dumb big guy who did everything "Snakes" told him to. He was an Eastender. I think he may have been on your list, too? A big fella, Colin Bell?'

'Yes. That's right.'

Posie stabbed at the list of names and found "Bell. C".

She scribbled her new information down on her blotting paper.

Olli Onneri is Snakes Hunter.

Matt Jenkins is Colin Bell.

'What happened to them, Len?'

'What always happens. They were legendary a few years ago, almost famous in the criminal underworld, but these lads got too big for their boots.'

Len explained that the two men had been caught in the act of safe-breaking, carted off by the police and sentenced to a spell in prison.

'This was around about 1921, I suppose. In York. But they'd already committed one of the biggest safe-cracking feats known in English history in 1920, and they got away with it! They robbed the English National Bank in Bath, emptied all the safes there of cash and valuables, and disappeared with the loot. Hid it somewhere. I suppose the whereabouts is still a secret.'

Posie supposed it was the Bath money that had been used at the Ritz, and she guessed it would have been keeping the pair in the lap of luxury for a good long time.

'But I don't remember any of this in the newspapers, Len. And how come Richard didn't remember any of it? He's the Chief Commissioner for goodness' sake!'

Len tapped his finger against his nose.

'It was before Richard was Commissioner, wasn't it? This story was all hushed up. Completely. The Government apparently didn't want the story to get out, to let the nation feel concerned about their valuables, or worry about how safe their banks were! The Home Office didn't allow the police to publish the extent of the losses from Bath in 1920, either. I only knew about it all because I 'appened to be in York in 1921, on a big shadowin' case, and a drunk policeman I met in a pub up there told me that "Snakes" Hunter and his big pal had been caught at last. He had heard they were to be banged up out of sight in York Gaol after a closed court session. And last month, early November I think it was, in the tiny trade adverts and among the legal notices of the *Gazette*, I noticed their names again. It was a miniscule notice, and I think it was published by the Home Office. "Snakes" and his wingman were being released, early, for good behaviour. You know how I 'ave to read the *Gazette* from cover to cover when it comes out, Po?'

'Mnnn. Yes. For the divorce notices…'

'That's right. Well, sometimes you come across unexpected nuggets which the government or the police need to publish according to the law, but they want the notices to be 'buried' where no-one will notice. So they put them in the *Gazette*, where no-one will read them except idiots like me, eh? Then it stays uncontroversial. I expect your Richard wasn't involved in their closed trial back in 1921, or the government cover-up, but I expect he'll remember "Snakes" Hunter, if you mention the name to him.'

Posie got up and stood at her window, staring out at the black nothingness of the dark office buildings. Snow was still falling. She rested her head against the cold glass and thought hard.

So why had Onneri, as Posie still thought of him, had to die?

And why had he been warned of his death with a string of mirrors? Had it nothing to do with magic, and something to do with revenge?

Someone who had had a fortune stolen from Bath, perhaps, and who remained angry at the insufficient justice which had been meted out?

But what had mirrors to do with it all, if that was the case?

Posie stuck to facts for a minute, as she knew Richard always, always did.

She turned to Len, who was still smoking. 'Hear me out?'

'Go on.'

'If what we've pieced together is correct, it seems this chap "Snakes" was with Houdini in 1919, as part of a magic act here in London, certainly starting off at the Holborn Empire, although he definitely didn't want anyone to know that; saying instead he'd met Houdini in 1920. Then something sends "Snakes" off course and he changes trade and works as a safe-breaker; he gets very rich, gets caught, gets imprisoned. He's finally released, gets out his stash of money from wherever he hid it and then sets himself up as a magician again, and a very fancy one at that, living in splendour, able to afford the very best of everything, including fake passports. He puts up adverts, trading off his earlier connections with Houdini. He becomes Count Olli Onneri. He wants to be the best yet. And through it all, Onneri never, ever went to America.'

'No.'

'So, America was all a lie. And the weird thing is that Onneri's career went completely full-circle. That would be like me going back to being an ambulance driver again, now. I mean, why? I've never heard of such a thing!'

Len ground out his roll-up on a twist of paper on Posie's desk.

'Perhaps magic was a passion of "Snakes" Hunter: perhaps that was all he really ever wanted to do? And in order to finance it, he had to get money. Perhaps he was born poor, or he was unsupported?'

The scent of Len's tobacco lingered in the air around them. 'Anyhow, perhaps being a safe-breaker and a magician are not so very different, Posie? Both need skill and patience, and a ridiculous level of self-belief in your own technical ability.'

'I suppose so.'

She'd have to telephone Richard now, tell him what she

had found out. About the real identities of Onneri and Jenkins.

Not that it helped a jot with finding out who exactly had killed the magician. Or why.

If anything, finding out that the dead man was a high-level thief who had evaded the customary justice only opened the flood-gates of possibilities with regards to the number of suspects there could be.

But just then the telephone rang and both Len and Posie almost jumped out of their skins.

Posie answered the phone and heard a brisk no-nonsense American voice.

'New York calling, the Arthur Avenue Exchange. Do you accept the call?'

'Of course!'

Len yawned and slunk from the room, and then Ricky Di Maggio was on the telephone, he of the historical graffiti in the dressing-room, and Posie was hearing the whole sorry story.

About an incident that had occurred at exactly this time of year, six years before.

An incident that had changed his life forever.

* * * *

Chapter Eight

She needed to call Richard to tell him to stop wasting everyone's time. To stop Fox from engaging American journalists to find out how well-known Onneri had been in New York. It would prove a fruitless search. A dead end.

But before she did so she called through to Fleet Street again, to the *Associated Press*. Even with Ricky Di Maggio's story still ringing in her ears, she needed clarity, proof.

She needed more help.

'Sam Stubbs, please. Posie Parker here.'

'He's busy, Miss Parker.'

'Tell him I have a scoop for him. He'll want to know all about it. Otherwise, I call *The Times*. It's his call.'

'Very well.'

Within a couple of minutes Sam was on the line. 'Well? What is it now, Posie?'

'I'll give you the scoop of your life tomorrow, Sam, but I need your help right now.'

'Not more names for me to listen to?' He gave a theatrical groan.

'No. I've worked those out, thanks. This is a loose thread, something really weird. Can you or one of your chaps take a look for me?'

Sam mock-yawned down the line. 'I'm listening. Although I wish I wasn't.'

'Can you check in your archives for me? The 18th or 19th December, 1919. Did anything really weird happen then? Here in London? But can you check the same date for Canterbury, too?'

'The Cathedral town, in Kent?'

'That's right. If you don't find anything, perhaps you could call through to one of your colleagues down there? Perhaps something odd made the local papers on the same dates?'

'Define "odd".'

'I can't. I'll know it when I hear it.'

'It's past eleven o'clock at night, Posie. Us poor London saps might be hard at it still, but those journalists out in the provinces will be safely tucked up in their beds. Lucky blighters!'

'First thing tomorrow, then? You can come over for this scoop after lunch.'

'Where?'

'The foyer of the Holborn Empire. One-thirty sharp.'

'Classy.'

'I always am. Until then. But ring me if you find anything out. Straightaway.'

Posie was at her bookcase again, and this time she had an old ecclesiastical book out, a survivor of the purge made on her father's small library after his death.

It was a directory of all benefices and churches within England, including telephone numbers.

She flicked it open.

Here it was, *Canterbury*.

There were over three hundred churches and church buildings listed for the one city. She had no time for that. She'd have to go straight to the very top.

She circled the telephone exchange number for the Cathedral's own Chapter House, and vowed she'd ring it first thing in the morning.

She also consulted her pocket map of London, and

circled the King's Cross Road. What had Di Maggio said? *Albert House*?

He'd remembered it because his brother was called Alberto, and he never forgot a name.

And now to track down Richard, and tell him what she'd found out.

Posie asked to be connected to his office at New Scotland Yard, but got no reply. She asked for Sergeant Fox instead.

Sergeant Fox answered the telephone, tiredness creeping through with every word.

'Yes, Miss?'

'Is my husband there, Sergeant?'

'He's just left. Said he was heading home.'

'I'd stop whatever you are doing, Sergeant. Get your men to look in the East End for a fella called Bell. Colin Bell.'

'Bell?'

'That's right. Find his parents' house and you'll probably find him. And stop researching America, too. It doesn't help us. You don't need to worry about tracing Miss Wheeler's pound notes, either. I know where they are from. And talking of Miss Wheeler, make sure she is able to come over to the theatre again tomorrow. At one-thirty sharp. She'll need some smart clothes on; she'll be photographed. We'll need Miss Peterson, too, and Colin Bell when you find him. Everyone needs to be back at the Holborn Empire tomorrow. I've invited Sam Stubbs there, too.'

'What? But why?'

'You'll be arresting Colin Bell for murder, Sergeant. Can you clear it all with the Manager, Mr Gulliver? Or his assistant, Loxley? Perhaps he'd like to come along and watch, too?'

'Of course.' Fox sounded relieved, and he bade Posie a quick good night.

There was nothing much more to do tonight, other than wait for the threads of the outstanding information to come in, and Posie got ready to go home.

Len had fallen asleep again in front of the dying embers of the fire, and she half-envied him his solitary rest, a bottle of Christmas sherry at his side, but she plodded on, on through Bloomsbury, through the falling snow, thinking of a story which had an almost-answer now.

A perfect ending.

But it was an ending which came six years too late.

* * * *

PART THREE

Saturday 19th December, 1925

(The Holborn Empire)

Chapter Nine

The snow had stopped and London was freshly-born again in purest white.

The sun shone.

Groups of carol singers thronged the touristy areas of Covent Garden, and a big Christmas tree market had been set up there. Braces of geese and ducks were being trundled on carts through the streets away from Smithfield, destined for the hotels and restaurants of Mayfair.

Over at the Holborn Empire, workmen on ladders pulled the last of the gold-spangled banners down, and new white posters advertising the upcoming Christmas show were being pasted up.

It was almost half-past one, and Posie waited nervously at the door of the Empire's foyer, peering out. She wore a black drop-waisted suit-dress with white buttons down the front, all in a row. Black for a funeral, white for the snow which covered up secrets.

A ring of seats and stools had been assembled by Rainbird, and these were occupied by Mr Gulliver's assistant, Loxley, by Miss Peterson, and by Colin Bell, the big man previously known as Matt Jenkins.

Colin Bell had been found safe and well in the bosom of his family home in the East End, together with Count

Onneri's blue leather duffle bag, and hundreds of pounds worth of brand-new bank notes, together with fake identity papers and a huge hoard of the purest cocaine, and all manner of other items of interest to the police.

Bell had shaved off his big black beard and shaved his hair clean away in an attempt at a fresh start and inconspicuousness, but he was unquestionably the same man.

He looked sweaty and surly and frightened now, and he sat in handcuffs, which no amount of magic would be able to free him from.

Dotted about the foyer were Constable Smallbone, Doctor Poots and Inspector Oats. A few other bobbies were ranged around the edges. Sam Stubbs was loitering in a corner, puffing away constantly on a pathetic excuse for a self-rolled cigarette.

Outside, a gleaming black police-car rolled up.

Out of the front passenger side hopped Richard Lovelace, wearing his formal Chief Commissioner's uniform, and the sun danced across the smart gold buttons, making them gleam against the navy gabardine of his dress jacket. Out of the back of the motor came Minnie Wheeler, handcuffed and accompanied by Sergeant Fox, but Posie was pleased to see she looked smart in a borrowed blue suit and freshly-applied make-up.

When they came in, Posie saw Richard was holding a cream-coloured telegram, which he passed across to her quickly. 'For you? I think it must have been sitting at the front-desk of the Yard all night and got ignored…'

She couldn't quite ignore the slight anger which prickled about Richard like a starchy halo, for he understandably felt that Posie had stolen his case away from underneath him, running away with it in her own manner.

But at least I am right, she thought to herself, ripping open the envelope and reading the telegram inside.

She breathed a sigh of relief.

Yes.

I am right.

Richard had sat down in the circle, as had Minnie Wheeler, in her handcuffs, next to Fox.

Posie sat down too, next to her husband, whose crossed arms and slightly hostile stance made her feel a million, billion miles away from him.

But Posie had to begin.

'Thank you for coming, everyone. We are here because of what happened yesterday, the murder of Count Onneri. But we are here for more than that, too. Because this case is really all about *stealing*. It's about magic, of course. And it's also about poor children, wanting to do better for themselves; pulling themselves up out of the gutter. But the crucial point is that it's mainly about stealing: stealing, in particular, a magic trick, which led on to all sorts of other stealing. Including, at the very end, stealing of a life.'

Posie looked straight at Colin Bell, who looked sharply away.

'Matt Jenkins here is really called Colin Bell. And neither he nor his friend, who re-named himself Count Olli Onneri, for reasons I will explain shortly, have ever been to America. Not alone, not together, and certainly *not* with Harry Houdini.'

Minnie Wheeler gasped, and the handcuffs jangled in her lap. 'No way! So there was no blimmin' Houdini connection at all?'

Posie put a hand up, as if to stop a tide of traffic.

'I didn't say that, exactly. Count Onneri's real name was Gerald Hunter. As a boy, despite being puny, he'd excelled at anything technical and mechanical, and seemed to be able to unpick a lock just by looking at it. He'd been intrigued by magic all his life; it was an escape for him. And one of his two main fascinations, from boyhood, was Harry Houdini. I suppose, but I don't know for sure, that both Hunter and Bell here answered an advert to be "stage hands" when Houdini decided to start his tour of England in December 1919. Houdini recruited a small team from scratch. Hunter and Bell must have met each other for the first time then, as part of that team, and carried on as a double-act thereafter. They have certainly always linked their fortunes, for good and for bad, to each other, ever since 1919. Until yesterday, they were inseparable.'

Sam Stubbs called out across the room, notepad at the ready: 'So Colin Bell was taken on by Houdini for his brute strength? And Gerald Hunter for his technical abilities?'

Posie grinned. 'Yes, something like that. They actually started the tour *here*, at the Holborn Empire. There was a core team including Harry Houdini as the main draw, of course. The others included the following: his wife who worked as a stage assistant; his theatrical manager, Jim Collins, and his set designer, Ricky Di Maggio. They all came across from America together. Houdini really needed another female stage assistant here though, and he hired one in London: a Miss Eliza Dean. This team worked well at the start of it all, and in fact they were photographed together, in full make-up and costume. See here?'

Posie went across to the wall, pointed at the photograph of the group there. 'May I?' she said quietly to Mr Loxley and he nodded sincerely. She took down the photograph and then passed it around the group.

Richard Lovelace studied it intently. 'Who is who?'

'The Houdinis are self-explanatory, but the girl-clown is Eliza Dean, and her opposite number, the sad clown in white, is Gerald Hunter, or, as we knew him yesterday, Count Olli Onneri. I suppose he occasionally came on stage to assist with magic tricks, in a background capacity. One of the big bulky Pierrots is Ricky Di Maggio, and the other is Colin Bell here. Those two men were almost the same size, which was handy for any tricks involving weights, or requiring the appearance of "doubles". Jim Collins, who still works for Houdini, does not come into our story once, not back then, and not now. Even though he is in this photograph.'

Posie sat down next to her husband. 'But things were starting to go very wrong here with this group. And not through any fault of Harry Houdini's. But he sensed it.'

Posie pointed again at the picture of him on his own on the wall. 'He says it was "*The Strangest Time of all!*"'

'What was wrong?' asked Mr Loxley, looking mildly concerned, as if the theatre itself might be at fault.

Posie had a notebook and the telegram all balanced in a pile on her lap and she grabbed at them now, as if for reassurance.

'The wrong was all due to one person: Gerald Hunter. He was wrong to the core. And while he would later acquire the nickname of "Snakes" Hunter, he was slippery and cunning and cruel enough even back in 1919 to create problems in such a tight-knit team.'

Inspector Oats piped up at once: 'Count Onneri was actually "Snakes" Hunter? But that's downright mad! Is this correct, Chief Commissioner?'

'That's right, Inspector.'

Richard looked green about the gills as he explained: 'I was only informed of this development late last night; a development which has since been confirmed by Ministers from the Home Office. Dental records have now proved the identity; that Count Onneri and "Snakes" Hunter are one and the same person. I have also been informed that some of the money we have recovered at the Ritz Hotel was stolen during a bank raid in Bath, back in 1920, and I am also now aware of the way-too lenient imprisonment of both Hunter and Bell, which ended one month ago.'

But Minnie Wheeler was clinging to the original story, desperate for some resolution about the man who had employed her. 'What happened back then, Miss Parker? Six years ago? With Houdini, here in 1919?'

Posie opened her notebook, flicked to the correct page.

'My source for unravelling this tale, and this murder, is not here. But he was very much here six years ago, in December 1919. He'd come over from America as a favour to Harry Houdini.'

'Ricky Di Maggio?' asked Richard, slightly less crossly than before.

Posie nodded. She pointed at the slightly bigger of the two Pierrot dolls in the photograph.

'He'd worked with Houdini for a few years, but he was tired of all the travelling and he wanted to work on Broadway again, to be nearer his tight-knit, Italian family. He'd agreed with Harry Houdini to set the British show up, work the first month, then return to New York. That was his plan...'

Posie saw how Colin Bell shifted in his seat unhappily, refusing to look up.

'Some of you have may have seen Ricky's words on the wall in an old, shared dressing-room downstairs. The words were painted on the wall when he was drunk, apparently, but the meaning was deadly serious: a warning given to others not to touch or take things from the cupboard. It was where Houdini's paperwork about his tricks were kept.'

'Had there been problems with thefts?' asked Sam Stubbs, writing hurriedly, barely looking up.

'Yes. Unsurprisingly, the problems were caused by Gerald Hunter. He was obsessed with Houdini and wanted to become a magician in his own right. He started stealing bits of mechanisms, just to see how it all worked. Di Maggio told me on the telephone that Houdini was at his wit's end; told Di Maggio to build a special cupboard chock-full of locks in Di Maggio's own shared dressing-room, and then to keep Houdini's most secret tricks inside of it during the run here. Which is what happened. The evidence is still downstairs.'

'But you've said Gerald Hunter was an expert at picking locks,' said Miss Peterson quietly, in consternation. 'So how was that effective?'

'It wasn't.'

Posie explained that Gerald Hunter attempted to pick the locks on the cupboard to see how easy it would prove to be.

'Unluckily for him, he was observed by the female assistant, Eliza Dean, who also shared the dressing-room. She saw him reflected in the mirror, as she was applying her stage make-up, and Gerald Hunter had the decency to put whatever he had taken out of the cupboard back into it.'

'What was the problem, then?' asked Sam Stubbs, looking up, frowning.

'The trouble was that little Eliza Dean ragged on Gerald Hunter anyway, and told everyone what she had seen. About his ability to unpick the locks.'

Posie paused in the telling of her tale, checked her notebook carefully before continuing.

'And then Gerald Hunter stole Houdini's magic mirror trick out of that locked cabinet a few days later anyway, unobserved, and on that occasion literally all hell broke loose. It was the end of the team.'

'You mean the same trick we saw yesterday, Posie?' demanded Richard Lovelace. 'The periscope? *That* trick was Houdini's?'

Posie nodded. 'Nearly all of Count Onneri's show yesterday was originally Houdini's. Tricks copied or stolen from Houdini in December 1919: "*The Strangest Time*".'

'Where are we going with all of this, darling?' hissed Richard impatiently, under his breath, but Posie wouldn't be hurried.

'As I said, when Gerald Hunter *did* succeed in opening that locked cabinet again, and stealing the trick, all hell broke loose.'

'What happened?' asked Miss Peterson, agog, right on the edge of her chair.

'Would you like to take over from me, Mr Bell?' asked

Posie politely. 'After all, you are the only one of us who was *actually* there on that fateful night...'

But the man shook his head and simply stared down at his handcuffs.

Posie read from her notes. 'Ricky Di Maggio told me he did a very bad thing: he has always regretted it since, even though he painted a warning on the wall. When Eliza Dean warned him about Hunter, Di Maggio placed a canister of acid inside the locked cabinet, very precariously, so that whoever forced it open would get acid all over themselves. Well, of course Gerald Hunter did exactly that and his hands took the brunt of the stuff. Di Maggio says he will regret it until his dying day.'

There were gasps all around.

Sam Stubbs was scribbling furiously and Oats was shaking his head in disbelief.

'Why was Count Onneri – I mean Mr Hunter – murdered yesterday, though?' asked Miss Peterson, in her low, sad voice, obviously moved.

'Surely, however badly he behaved all those years ago, stealing didn't warrant being murdered?' Miss Peterson sounded perplexed, sad. 'It sounds like he got his punishment, the burns? And that was terrible enough.'

Posie shuffled her notes.

'I said this case was about stealing. It's really about the *repercussions* of stealing. There was another story going on here, too. All along. A sort of rags-to-riches story.'

A failed fairy-tale.

Posie picked up the photograph of the 1919 team again, tapped very lightly the picture of the girl clown, in her white outfit.

'Eliza Dean was extraordinarily beautiful, apparently. It was the reason she got the job here, ahead of hundreds of other hopeful girl applicants. Do you remember I said this case was also about poor children? Well, Eliza was one of those. She'd got herself away from the London Orphanage where she'd been abandoned as a child in the East End, and she'd worked incredibly hard over several years, mainly as a fashion model and shop assistant, but what she really wanted to do was be on the stage. She answered Houdini's advert to work with him. He wanted a beautiful young assistant who would be game for everything: knife-throwing; being sawn in half; being submerged in tanks. Eliza took the job to further her ambition of being on the stage. But she knew that wasn't enough: she knew she needed a bit of luck; a bit of stardust. Here, at the Holborn Empire she thought she'd found it in the shape of Ricky Di Maggio.'

Richard harrumphed beside her and Inspector Oats rolled his eyes impatiently.

'They got together? Got married? Eloped?' Sam Stubbs was impatient too, but greedily snapping up all the details he was offered.

'None of those things.'

Posie described a hot-house feeling, of emotions rising. Of the girl, the white clown, Eliza Dean, sensing an opportunity with Di Maggio, who was shortly to return to his native city.

'Ricky Di Maggio adored Eliza, and he invited her to New York. He promised they would marry there, and he would make her the star of a Broadway show. It must have been the answer to all of Eliza's prayers, and we know she was getting everything ready to go. She'd applied for all the correct boat passes; resigned from Houdini's show here. Eliza was probably not in love with Di Maggio, as he himself admits today, but the story could have shifted that way if things had turned out differently. *If* she had gone away with him.'

'I'm not followin' you,' said Minnie Wheeler, confused. 'Did something 'appen to the white girl clown? To Miss Dean?'

'Yes.'

Posie let the silence in the room beat on, thick as unshed tears.

'Eliza Dean vanished, Miss Wheeler. Right into thin air. Last night, on the telephone, Ricky Di Maggio told me it was December 18th, the same day as yesterday, six years ago, when Eliza disappeared. She'd had a day off, then she simply didn't turn up for work anymore; leaving all her clothes and papers behind in the dressing-room here. Di Maggio said it was uncharacteristic of Eliza, but he admitted he'd only known her a short time: a couple of weeks; it had been a whirlwind romance. When he raised the alarm and called the police they refused to investigate, said a girl like Eliza was "two a penny". Houdini himself pleaded for help, but no help came.'

Sam Stubbs, a cigarette now balanced precariously, waved an old newspaper in the air.

'I can confirm that there is no mention in any of the London newspapers of Eliza Dean, or of her disappearance in December 1919. It's as if she never existed.'

Richard was nettled, slightly shocked: 'What are you suggesting, Posie? That "Snakes" Hunter, and perhaps this big bully-boy Bell here killed Eliza? Or got rid of her in some way?'

Posie nodded. She felt on the verge of very sudden tears.

A whole life scrubbed out, just like that.

'It was *not* Ricky Di Maggio who Gerald Hunter blamed for the excruciating acid burns he suffered. Ricky was clear about that on the telephone. *I* believe that Gerald Hunter blamed the beautiful girl, Eliza Dean. Hunter blamed her personally for watching him in the mirror and for the acid which was put in the cupboard as a direct result of her reporting him. I reckon he blamed Eliza directly for the ghastly damage to his hands, which would last forever, and possibly spoil his chances as a magician. Perhaps Gerald Hunter was also jealous of Eliza's bright future, of her planned trip to New York? Perhaps, unless Mr Bell here speaks, we will never know the truth.'

Everyone stared at Colin Bell but he concentrated on the floor and didn't move a muscle.

Posie dashed her hand past her eyes, made it look like she was moving her hair, rather than wiping away tears.

'I think Hunter and Bell carried on for a bit here with Houdini after Eliza's disappearance, but Houdini got rid of them when his tour moved north, probably with some relief. Then they went quiet for a bit. Don't forget, Hunter was unable yet to work as the magician he so wanted to be: he had no arsenal of funds to get a show up and running. Besides, his hands needed to heal. He and Bell focused instead on robbery and safe-cracking. They needed money. And speaking of money, it's very strange, but Eliza Dean had been carefully assembling a bank account, to see her prudently through the rest of her life, and after the 18th December 1919 it was never touched again. It was her pride and joy, according to Di Maggio. But it *was* touched one month ago, when a cheque was drawn from it to pay for the use of this theatre, for last night's show: for a booking of one night only.'

Sergeant Fox was shaking his head in disbelief: 'What are you talking about, Miss Parker?'

The Sergeant was almost up on his feet now, half-dragging Minnie Wheeler up with him. 'If Eliza *is* dead, who wrote the cheque, and why? An avenger?'

'No,' said Posie, slowly.

'Much better than that.'

****

Chapter Ten

She looked all around for effect.

'I spoke of poor children, an orphanage. Well, it turns out that Eliza Dean was not alone in the orphanage. She had a little sister. Fifteen years old, back in 1919. Di Maggio told me on the telephone that this little sister was Eliza's pride and joy: that she had worked hard to get her and her sister out of the orphanage; paid for a flat on the King's Cross Road for them to share as a home.'

Posie flicked through her notes. 'Eliza told Di Maggio she wouldn't leave London without this girl, because her sister needed to be specially looked after. Di Maggio assumed the girl was simple, very child-like, and would need support in her life in America. All of which Di Maggio promised and agreed to.'

Minnie Wheeler clapped a hand over her mouth: 'Oh poor soul! Did he take her back with him anyway?'

Posie shook her head.

'It didn't turn out like that. The day Di Maggio noticed Eliza was missing, the sister turned up here at the Theatre. It was the first time she'd met Di Maggio. He said there was hardly any resemblance between the sisters, virtually nothing: it was almost uncanny how the two could be so different. And uncanny how young the sister looked;

years younger than fifteen. Like a child! But Eliza's sister impressed him with her passion: she was like a firework; screamed the place down. Kicked over chairs, hit the walls. The sister blamed Di Maggio personally for Eliza's disappearance. She screamed at him that Eliza had told her she'd been invited on a special date with Di Maggio. To Canterbury, in the South, and Eliza had gone, all dressed up and looking wonderful, hopeful of an engagement ring. But Eliza had never returned. The fifteen-year-old said she knew something was wrong: Eliza would never leave her. She claimed she would avenge Eliza, if it was the last thing she ever did.'

Posie tailed off.

She was remembering the kindly voice of the American on the telephone last night. His sad, plaintive drawl:

'I told the kid I had no idea what she was talking about. Hell, why would I have invited Eliza to a place I'd never been to? I mean, where is Canterbury, anyway? We had all of London on our doorstep; why would I have taken Eliza anywhere else? We liked to go to a bakery that sold cream cakes; Fritzi's, it was called. That suited us fine.'

He'd grown melancholy at the remembrance:

'Anyhow, this kid was beating her fists on me and tears were running down that little face of hers and I thought both our hearts might break. I guess then I knew something was wrong. I pulled out the boat tickets I had booked for us three, and I even showed her the diamond ring I had bought for her sister, but hadn't yet had a chance to propose with...and then she ran off. I never saw the kid again; I swear to God.'

Lovelace covered his face briefly with his hands and Posie heard him groan softly to himself.

'So, we *do* have an avenger on our hands?' he said, sitting up again, calm as you like. 'An avenger who is also a sister.'

'I believe so,' said Posie, equally calmly.

She carried on: 'I suppose that Eliza's sister must have gone home and tried to puzzle things out. Di Maggio's sincerity must have impressed her, and she must, over time, have come to the conclusion that Gerald Hunter was, in fact, the man to blame for Eliza's disappearance. Eliza had probably spoken about seeing Gerald Hunter reflected in their mirror, breaking open the cupboard; the sister must have heard about the revenge of Di Maggio's acid trick. The sister must have known Eliza was uneasy about her fellow-colleague, Gerald: that he was a strange, creepy sort. Perhaps, when she'd figured all this out and gone to confront Gerald, she found that he and his friend Bell had moved on? Or perhaps she was simply thinking things out and biding her time? Without any confrontation.'

Posie passed her husband the telegram she had received, and he read it quickly.

Posie read from her notebook again.

'But Ricky Di Maggio was wrong about something. And that was to assume Eliza's sister needed special care because she was child-like. That was absolutely *not* the case. Eliza's sister needed special care because she was quite brilliant, technically and academically. But also because she was quite dangerous. Almost mad with genius, in fact. Or else, just mad. Plain and simple.'

Richard had paled beneath his usual freckled creamy pallor, and he cast a quick glance over at Colin Bell, then at Minnie Wheeler.

A subtle inflexion of the head brought two of the bobbies closer to the circle, with Richard indicating they should stand behind Bell and Miss Wheeler.

'Dangerous?' demanded Sam Stubbs, on edge, agog. 'Mad? How so?'

Posie had done a little research.

She'd gone to King's Cross, and found out that Albert House was at number 8 on the King's Cross Road, WC1. She'd spoken to the porter there who had been very helpful: he'd given her the name of the Landlord. Who she'd then rung up from her office.

'I tried to piece together a history. I found out that Miss Eliza Dean and her sister had lived at a flat in Albert House, WC1, since the middle of the Great War. After Eliza's disappearance in 1919, her sister has continued living there, paying the rent on time every week. There have occasionally been complaints made about noises, and smells, and smoke, all coming from the flat. Strange smells, blacked-out windows. Explosions, sometimes. There were rumours of experiments, or that the occupier was a photographer. But the Landlord doesn't care as long as he gets his money on time. However, the most interesting thing the Landlord *could* tell me was that during the Great War, he received part of the rent paid straight from a Government Armaments factory, on Sumner Street in Southwark, where grenades and small explosive armaments were made. And that was the place Eliza Dean's sister worked at as part of the war effort.'

Lovelace again groaned.

Posie continued: 'It was the work of a few minutes for me to investigate. It turns out that the younger Miss Dean worked at the factory from the age of twelve, stopping in 1917. She was expressly recommended to the Armaments factory, as the orphanage claimed she had shown real genius at school. Especially in science and mechanics. The trouble was that she got bored easily...'

Posie explained that there had been several instances at the Southwark factory where devices had been set off, probably deliberately, or wired up deliberately wrongly in order to create big explosions.

One such explosion had caused a massive fire.

People had died.

The devices each time had been traced back to Eliza Dean's sister, and after the big fire she had been asked to leave. She was let go.

It had been dangerous but ultimately boring work for a mind so unique.

'I suppose Miss Dean has carried on with her own scientific experiments at home, and hence all the bangs and smoke,' explained Posie to the group. 'I can find no other trace for her in any registered employment of any kind to date. The trail is cold for Miss Petra Dean, for that is her name. Oh, apart from *this*...'

Posie passed the telegram around to everyone in the group, although Colin Bell did not take it, or attempt to.

It said:

'MISS PARKER,

I'M SENDING THIS DIRECT TO SCOTLAND YARD AS I BELIEVE IT IS THE MIDDLE OF YOUR NIGHT RIGHT NOW!

I CONFIRM GERALD HUNTER WAS EFFECTIVE IN STEALING DETAILS OF MY MAGIC TRICKS FROM ME. I AM GLAD MY MIRROR TRICK WAS SO SUCCESSFUL; I HAVE NOT AS YET TRIED IT OUT MYSELF: IT SEEMED TAINTED SOMEHOW.

I ALSO CONFIRM I HAVE NO NIECES LIVING IN ENGLAND AND CERTAINLY NONE NAMED PETERSON!

KIND REGARDS,

HARRY HOUDINI'

Lovelace stood up, sadness pressing around his shoulders like a heavy weight.

He turned to face the secretary in her smart purple clothes.

'Miss Peterson? *You* are Eliza Dean's younger sister?'

A silence, then a nod.

'You are Petra Dean? Did *you* clear out her bank account to book this theatre?'

Another nod.

'And did you send those messages with strychnine on the mirrors?'

Another nod.

'And did you rig the mirror on stage yesterday with a live circuit of electricity so it was dangerous upon touch?'

'Yes. That's right.' The voice was loud and very proud.

The young girl suddenly stood up, and she seemed much taller than before.

Her ugly green eyes blazed with a fire which Posie hadn't seen there previously. The girl didn't shout, but the loud words she was emitting were getting faster, frenzied:

'I'm proud my sister ragged on Gerald Hunter after she saw what he was up to, and I'm glad I finished him off for good yesterday. He was an utterly dreadful person, especially now that he believed he was a "true" magician. "*Count Onneri*"! What stupid kind of name is that? The arrogance! I'm glad he suffered. He suffered with the burns six years ago, and he suffered with yesterday's electric shock. He was probably suffering already from strychnine ingestion, and I hope he felt dreadful, every single minute he was up on that wretched stage…'

Petra Dean laughed and it was an eerie sound. It was completely without sympathy or forgiveness.

'I decided long ago that I'd get Gerald Hunter in any way I could. I followed his progress as a criminal; I tracked him down to that prison in York where he was serving a pathetically secret term, having never been tried by a proper Judge or Jury. I've got by on my own all these years - since Eliza left - by making medicines; distilling drugs up in my flat, and selling them for good money. With that money I paid a Prison Warder there to tell me when Hunter would be released, and then I vowed I'd serve him up with *real* justice. And it was a godsend when I realised Hunter would be coming back to London, with a new name, to try and claim some sort of misguided glory as a magician here! His ultimate ambition! I decided to try to become part of Count Onneri's team; to get him back to this place, in any way I could. That was my one and only aim. It was the work of a moment to have a fake telegram sent to me from America, saying I was Houdini's niece. It would be a golden ticket in, for sure. I knew Onneri wouldn't question it a bit. Or check it. How could he?'

The girl's voice got faster now, excited to share her tale; her ingeniousness.

'When I found out the Holborn Empire was vacant on the anniversary of Eliza's disappearance it seemed as if it was meant to be. I paid for it with Eliza's money; it was *her* revenge, after all, wasn't it? And then I pretended to Count Onneri that the theatre was given for free. I must have been quite convincing. It was *me* who set up the old, shared dressing-room as being the only one available, because that is where everything happened, and you should have seen his face when he entered the place again. It was a picture!'

'And why did you send the mirrors?' Posie asked softly.

'I wanted to taunt him. Eliza had seen him in the mirror, you see, and that was her undoing. So now he would wonder if these mirrors would be *his* undoing, too. I liked the way it unsettled him. I even used Eliza's own hand-mirror that she used to keep here in the dressing-room. Perhaps he recognised it? I hope it made him think of her, and how lovely she was. The wretched ruddy little coward!'

Petra Dean shrugged.

'Poison was okay, it was a good start, and easy for me to distil myself, but Hunter needed to be gone quicker than that. In a more certain manner. I debated about poisoning his stashes of cocaine, but I couldn't be certain it would be a bad enough death. No: he deserved to fry to death. And if it was in front of people, and if he was scared by a little campaign of nasty, poisoned messages beforehand, then so much the better. I told you, Miss Parker, didn't I? That I've always been fascinated by magic. Well, I'm certainly handy enough to know how to short-circuit some electrics. I did that for years at the ammunitions factory! Yes: anyone can stick on a false beard and dye their hair, and anyone can steal someone else's magic tricks, but you have to be born good and beautiful, like my sister was. Everything was taken from her, all in one go. And taken from *me*, too. We were about to embark on a whole new life and it was ripped away from us both. How is that fair? And so now I've done the same to Hunter. I've got revenge for both me and my sister. And good riddance! I was so excited about killing him yesterday that I was shaking all day; not out of nerves, like Hunter believed, but out of pure excitement.'

Posie felt a shiver trickle down her spine, but there was a mad logic about the girl's reasoning; that much was true.

Richard gestured for Rainbird to take Miss Peterson from the room and for her rights to be read out to her.

But rather than protest, Petra Dean stuck her thin, bony arms out willingly, rather pathetically.

Petra Dean had been sat next to Colin Bell throughout, but hadn't so far said a word to him. And now she smiled sweetly down at the shaved, downturned head and she spat at him violently.

He barely moved.

'I know you had a part in all this,' Petra Dean said, clearly. 'Perhaps it was you who even killed her? But you obviously haven't got a brain in your worm-like head at all, so I expect you were just following *his* orders. I'd feel sorry for you if I had time to, but I expect they'll hang me as soon as ever they can. No secret prison terms for little Petra, eh?'

And when she had gone, everyone stared at the big man who was still sitting motionless.

'I suggest to you, Mr Bell,' said Posie in a measured

voice, 'that you and Mr Hunter went down to Canterbury, didn't you? On Eliza's day off, on the 18th December, 1919? Mr Hunter must have tricked her somehow into believing she was invited down there by her American suitor…'

At the complete silence which met her questions, Richard interjected: 'Why Canterbury, though, Posie? What put you onto that?'

The only reason Posie knew about Canterbury being important in all of this was a throwaway comment Di Maggio had made last night, when he'd said Petra was convinced Eliza was going to Canterbury on their supposed date.

It was specific, and strange enough to merit investigation.

'I guessed that Onneri – or Hunter, as he was – must have had a connection with Canterbury. So, I dug around.'

Posie had started by ringing the Chapter House of the Cathedral, asking if the name of Gerald Hunter was on any of the city's lists of baptisms, or choirs, or Sunday Schools from when he had been a boy, about twenty years back.

It had been a stab in the dark, but she'd got lucky and the results had been illuminating. She explained what she had found out.

'Gerald Hunter, who became Count Onneri, was yet another poor child, of a background remarkably similar to that of the Dean sisters. He grew up at the main Canterbury City Orphanage, but, like Petra Dean, his talents were recognised and he was dispatched off to the Cathedral itself once or twice a week by the Head of the Orphanage, at the age of twelve or thirteen, probably with the hope of securing future employment there. Gerald Hunter was told to make himself handy and to fix things in the Cathedral. I spoke to one of the Cathedral vergers, who had known Gerald Hunter as a boy. And what he said was telling…'

Posie explained that Gerald Hunter had been useful at the Cathedral, undoubtedly, but he'd whizz through the tasks given to him and then mooch around for hours.

And *where* he'd mooch was at the tomb of the Black Prince, high up in the Cathedral, a tomb as ancient and gilded and gorgeous as you might ever find, just about anywhere in the world.

'He liked to hang about by this dark tomb for a dark warrior. A warrior with a questionable reputation.'

'The Black Prince? Who's he when he's at home?' muttered Oats, rather nastily, mockingly.

Richard laughed, a little less tense now. 'He's England's very own nasty piece of work,' he explained. 'A classic Knight who slaughtered thousands in long-ago wars, and got a 'black' reputation for his efforts. Bit of a showman, I seem to remember. Lots of gold and finery on his tomb in Canterbury. Isn't that right, Posie darling?'

Posie agreed. 'Apparently our boy Gerald Hunter was as fascinated with the Black Prince as he was with Houdini. It was a real obsession: he devoured every history book going about the Prince; he'd hang around the Cathedral Treasury asking if he could polish the bronze of the tomb, or clean the gold leather lion which perched atop the tomb. He was also unhealthily attracted to a place outside the city which had been named after the Prince, a place known for magic. Eventually the Cathedral said they had no more use for Gerald; his mooching and his obsession got too much. But he carried that strange history with him forever. It stayed with him.'

'How so?' asked Richard, quizzically.

Posie wrote something quickly in her pad in big, stark letters.

'Petra Dean said she didn't understand Onneri's name, and that it was stupid. But puny little Gerald Hunter wanted to add some dark magic glamour to his own life when he emerged to become the magician of his dreams. He would find small ways of doing this, of course, like adopting the Black Prince's golden lion as his own motif, and having it stamped on his leather goods, and on his tickets to his shows. But he also wanted to make a big statement. He was obsessed by the Black Prince, wasn't he? And the Black Prince's symbol was the lion, and the Black Prince's language was French. So he combined all these things in one neat way.'

She held up her pad, where she had written:

LE LION NOIR

'Oh! How clever!' exclaimed Sergeant Fox.

'"THE BLACK LION" or "LE LION NOIR" becomes "OLLI ONNERI." It's an anagram, and a good one too.'

Much muttering ensued, and then Posie coughed.

She'd reached the end of things now.

'I tracked down the magic place associated with the Black Prince. It's a Well, just outside the city, at Harbledown. It was supposed to cure all ailments. It even cured the Black Prince himself, once upon a time.'

She stood and spoke directly to Colin Bell again.

'I suppose you pretended an invite for Eliza Dean had come from Ricky Di Maggio, did you? To that Well? An invitation she couldn't refuse? And then you dressed up smartly, to resemble Ricky Di Maggio. You were, after all, the same height and size as each other and you would have looked convincing from afar, or in the dark. You planned to meet Eliza there, and we *do* have evidence that she turned up.'

Sam Stubbs waved his newspaper again. He called out triumphantly:

'This 'ere is a Canterbury edition of the *Gazette* from 19th December 1919. It reports that a taxi-driver nearly lost his life in the fog of Harbledown Hill the day before, when his motor-car skidded. As part of the report, he claimed he had dropped off a girl matching Eliza's description at the Black Prince's Well. That it had seemed like she was waiting for someone to arrive. A man, probably…a date.'

Richard Lovelace got to his feet, stood right in front of Colin Bell, and Posie saw he had crossed his arms to stop himself from launching at the man.

'What did you do to Eliza? Or what did *Hunter* do to her, Bell? Or was it the two of you together, two bally dreadful men ganged up on one poor defenceless girl?' demanded Lovelace angrily, almost roaring.

'And what on earth did you do with Eliza's body, Bell?'

But Colin Bell had closed his eyes and was rocking slightly, utterly unreachable.

'We'll need evidence, sir! I think we'll have to send a team down to Kent and get them digging, sir, at this Black Prince's fancy little well, eh?' called out Inspector Oats, hopefully.

'Absolutely. Can you get onto that now, Bill? Head down South yourself and take charge if at all possible, eh?'

Oats, who liked nothing better than to be in charge, nodded happily. 'Right away, sir.'

Richard straightened up his Commissioner's cap, scowled, turning.

'Well, what a Christmas treat this has been, eh? One suspect arrested for a murder which took place yesterday, and another shortly to be arrested for a murder which took place years ago!'

Richard rolled his eyes. 'And both murders connected by that wretched mirror trick of old Houdini's, which he himself never even performed. Go on then, lads, grab Mr Bell, would you? If the blighter doesn't talk, he should take comfort in the fact that he'll swing for his crimes soon enough. There'll be no secret jail terms and private court sessions this time around, not with me in charge. You mark my words.'

Fox and Smallbone moved in on Colin Bell, whose

attempts to shake them off whilst in handcuffs were severely limited.

Lovelace started to talk quickly to Minnie Wheeler, apologising profusely, unlocking her handcuffs himself. He was shrugging, splaying his hands.

Dreadfully sorry. Who would have thought it, eh?

Posie went over to a window in the foyer and looked out at the packed snow on the ground outside.

She had a headache and felt as if the lights were flickering around her. She was also very hungry for lunch.

She hoped Richard could get away, otherwise she'd find some place to eat on her own near the British Museum. An Italian, perhaps. And she'd raise a glass to the helpful Ricky Di Maggio.

She thought of beautiful Eliza, probably under ice right now, undisturbed for six years. She thought of Eliza's ugly sister, Petra, riding in a police-car towards uncertainty.

Perhaps Petra would be able to plead some sort of madness, after all. Insanity? It didn't seem beyond the reach of probability.

Posie caught a salty tear with her tongue.

Suddenly Inspector Rainbird was beside her. She turned, smiling.

'Ah, Inspector Rainbird. And how is Prudence? I think she may not have been feeling well yesterday: I noticed she hadn't been in. Is she all right?'

And his face flushed in the blue reflected light of the snow outside, and Posie grinned.

She had guessed right.

A baby, then. What lovely news. Even if it wasn't being acknowledged yet.

'Prudence is fine, thank you, Miss. She'll be in after Christmas like usual, I expect.' He flushed an even brighter red, but hurried on: 'She had a little scare yesterday, actually. Had to get along to the hospital for a bit. But she's fine. Yes: all fine.'

'Glad to hear it, Inspector.'

Heaven knew they needed something jolly and warm just now, and nothing could beat news of a baby!

Posie felt delighted.

Rainbird pulled up the collar of his ludicrously thin coat. 'I'll be off now, then, Miss Parker. Brrr, it's cold in here now, isn't it? And the lights are awful here, too. They keep going on and off. Most inconvenient.'

'Yes, it is inconvenient. If I don't see you before, I hope you have a wonderful Christmas, and a fantastic New Year. Full of excitement.'

Excitement.

Well, they had had that in spades. Only a minute before, a woman in white had peered around the door from the auditorium, with large oversized pom-poms sewn onto her clown's jacket. It looked like the long-necked girl from the stage earlier, who had been putting rosin on the floor and waiting in the wings. She looked happy, but that could have been the clown's smile painted on her face.

A woman in white.

There was nothing gothic or ghostly about this girl, though; she seemed a helpful sort.

It was probably just the hired girl from the box-office, but nevertheless Posie had screwed up her eyes and willed the woman to go away. Breathed in and out several times over.

And when she'd looked back, there was nothing there. Just the cold still air, and the scent of Christmas on it, a promise of all the golden days to come, which they were lucky enough to hope for, and to have, stretching before them.

Tricks of the light.

Magic.

But there was no such thing as magic.

Lovelace came over and took his wife's arm. 'Lunch, I think,' he announced.

He tutted impatiently: 'Do you know, Loxley's been telling me the lights have all fused again. By Gad, what a wretched place. Let's get away. Never to return, eh? And well done, darling. As always, you were quite bally amazing. Even if I *was* cross that my supposed triumph was snatched away quite so forcibly. But I accept it: I got it wrong. You should definitely wear your little Sherlock Holmes coat out today, eh?'

'How funny you are, darling,' she smiled.

But he'd given her an idea.

Next week was Richard's birthday and in the absence of any other gifts, perhaps she's buy him a deerstalker, or a cape, or anything reminiscent of that Great Detective on Baker Street.

Perhaps even a small teddy bear with a Sherlock Holmes 'look' about him.

In fact, in the Canterbury newspaper from December 1919 which Sam Stubbs had presented her with earlier, before everyone else had arrived, she had seen a small advert for that very thing, a teddy bear made in Canterbury, and it had looked quite wonderful. Maybe she would call later that afternoon and check the company was still going, and place an order?

Or perhaps Posie and Richard would, in the next couple of days, have reason to go to Canterbury itself, to pay their respects to the girl who had been lost in all of this, and the visit would close the story down for good.

She'd arrange to go and buy a bear then, if she could sneak away for a bit.

Together Posie and Richard left the darkness of the Holborn Empire, and picked their way out through the snow. It was good to be outside again. Away from all of that.

Richard bent down all of a sudden and kissed her cheek tenderly.

She smiled.

There might not be magic, but there *was* such a thing as a good man.

And love.

Because that went on and on.

* * * *

Historical Note

All of the characters in this novella are fictional, unless specifically mentioned below.

Weather, timings, general political events, and places (and descriptions of places) are historically accurate to the best of my knowledge, save for any exceptions listed below.

As in the other Posie Parker books, I refer to the First World War of 1914–1918 as the 'Great War' throughout, which is simpler for the modern reader, although it would not have been referred to in this way in 1925.

As ever, Posie's work address in London (Grape Street, Bloomsbury, WC1) and her home address around the corner (Museum Chambers, WC1) are both very real, although you might have to do a bit of imagining to find her there.

A Brief Note on Characters

Harry Houdini (1874–1926) the real-life Hungarian-American magician and escape artist is referred to frequently in this novella although he never actually appears.

Houdini was the most famous stunt performer of his day, and was known as 'the handcuff king'. He is arguably still recognised as being the greatest escape artist and magician the world has ever seen. He was based in America, but came to London first in 1900 (where he gained notoriety by handcuffing himself to a pillar outside of New Scotland Yard, and then freeing himself again, thereafter securing himself a theatrical agent and a run at the Alhambra Theatre in Leicester Square). He toured in the United Kingdom frequently between 1900 until 1920, which year marked Houdini's final run of British shows. These took place over a six-month period and took in Edinburgh, Glasgow, Brighton and many other big towns. We know Houdini played the London Palladium for two weeks in May 1920 (earning the highest ever salary paid to one performer at that venue), and that he ended his tour at the New Cross Empire on June 12 1920, but there is some confusion as to whether he was already playing in London in December 1919.

For the sake of my plot I have used this grey area of doubtfulness and have placed my prologue during this potential winter visit.

Therefore, Houdini's run of shows at the Holborn Empire in December 1919 are a pure fiction on my part and did not ever happen.

Bess Houdini (1876–1943) was the American wife of Harry Houdini, and was also his stage assistant in real life, and accompanied him on his many trips to the United Kingdom. While there were many other stage assistants, Bess remained a constant.

Jim Collins was also a real assistant; a trusted mechanic who co-created many of Houdini's tricks and special effects.

Please note that Houdini's female assistant in this novella, Eliza Dean, and her own story, are entirely fictional. As is the character of Ricky Di Maggio, whose person and exploits are only real in my head.

The characters of Olli Onneri and Matt Jenkins are also both completely fictional.

1. (Prologue, and generally throughout) The Well of the Black Prince is indeed a real place, and is situated at Harbledown, just outside of Canterbury, in the South-East of England. It is, these days, an almost-unknown place, in contrast to how very important it was in the past, when it was famous.

   For more, see: https://www.pilgrimswaycanterbury.org/poi/black-princes-well/

   The Black Prince, Edward Woodstock (1330-1376) was never King of England, only heir apparent (king in waiting). He is famous for his dashing, glamourous image as a 'model' Knight, and for being one of the main commanders during the 'Hundred Year's War' between England and France, but he is equally famous for his gruesome, bloody deeds, which earned him the nickname of 'the Black Prince.' He long had an association with Canterbury, frequently travelling through the city on his way to France, but more so when he became desperately ill from dysentery abroad and sought help from miracles, and miraculous places.

   The Well at Harbledown is first recorded in 1081, and a leper hospital was built up and around it, as the Well was believed to have special curative waters. It is believed that Thomas Becket, Archbishop of Canterbury, lost a shoe in it, and after Becket was killed and became a martyr, thousands of pilgrims flocked to the Well *en route* to the Cathedral every year, anxious to 'take' its waters. The lost shoe was miraculously found and became an attraction all of its own!

Chaucer's fictional pilgrims came here, and Erasmus visited, being invited to kiss the holy shoe. We know that water from the Well was sent all over the medieval Kingdom to those who could not personally make the journey.

The association (and name, and the stone with the Black Prince's symbol upon it) dates from 1371, when the Prince 'took' the waters of the Well and supposedly got a good deal better, and he again 'took' water from the Well in 1376, when he was on his deathbed. He is buried in great state in Canterbury Cathedral, with a staggeringly over-the-top effigy atop his tomb, and where his original jacket, gloves, ceremonial hat (with a huge lion upon it) are still exhibited.

2. (Prologue) Despite what my taxi-driver says, the village-funded memorial to the twenty-seven young men from Harbledown, Canterbury, who died in the Great War was not in fact erected until May 1920.

3. (Throughout) The Holborn Empire is no more, having been demolished in the 1960s after extensive WWII damage from which it never really recovered. In its heyday, between the 1890s and the 1930s, the Holborn Empire was a cheap and cheerful theatre specialising in comedy and variety performances, and much later, films.

4. (Chapters Three, Four and Six) Olli Onneri's show at the Holborn Empire on 18 December 1925 is fictional, of course. The Managing Director, Charles Gulliver, who ran the London Theatres of Variety

Limited (which included thirty London music halls, including the Holborn Empire) was very real, and I include his name just for a touch of authenticity. His assistant, George Loxley, is fictional. There was never, to the best of my knowledge, any problem with any of the dressing-rooms at the Holborn Empire, nor superstition attached to anything or anyone there.

5. (Throughout) Although my Miss Peterson is fictional, Bess Houdini *did* have a sister, Marie, who married a John Hinson in 1911, the couple later going on to have their own daughter, Marie Hinson.

6. (Chapter Seven) Richard Enright (1871–1953) was a real-life person, and, as stated here, he was the Commissioner of the NYPD at the time of this novel. Michael Fiaschetti was also a real policeman, in charge of the prominent (and exceedingly dangerous) New York Italian Squad until 1922, when he then worked as a freelance detective for the New York Police.

7. (Chapter Nine) There *was* an Armaments Factory at Sumner Street in Southwark from 1915 onwards (known as 'Emergency Factory Number One') and for the duration of the Great War but the fire I mention is fictional. Fires in such factories were, however, sadly, fairly common.

8. (Chapter Nine) The 'Sherlock Holmes Bear' Posie has been advertised is fictional. However, whilst they were not operational in either 1919 or 1925, the truly wonderful company 'Canterbury Bears' make the best teddies in the world. I expect they would even make a Sherlock bear if you asked nicely.

You can find them here:
https://www.canterburybears.com/

Thank you for joining Posie Parker and her friends.

Enjoyed *Murder through the Mirror* (A Posie Parker Mystery #14)? Here's what you can do next.

If you loved this book and have a tiny moment to spare, I would really appreciate a review or rating on the page where you bought the book. Your help in spreading the word about the series is invaluable and really appreciated, and reviews make a big difference to helping new readers find the series.

Posie's other cases are available in e-book and paperback formats from Amazon, as well as in selected bookstores and at Audible and other main audiobook retailers. You can find all of the other books, available for purchase, listed here in chronological order:

http://www.amazon.com/L.B.-Hathaway/e/B00LDXGKE8

and

http://www.amazon.co.uk/L.B.-Hathaway/e/B00LDXGKE8

You can sign up to be notified of new releases, pre-release specials, free short stories, and the chance to win Amazon gift-vouchers here:

http://www.lbhathaway.com/newsletter/

About the Author

Cambridge-educated, British-born L.B. Hathaway writes historical fiction. She worked as a lawyer at Lincoln's Inn in London for almost a decade before becoming a full-time writer. She is a lifelong fan of detective novels set in the Golden Age of Crime, and is an ardent Agatha Christie devotee.

Her other interests, in no particular order, are: very fast downhill skiing, theatre-going, drinking strong tea, Tudor history, exploring castles and generally trying to cram as much into life as possible.

The Posie Parker series of cosy crime novels span the 1920s. They each combine a core central mystery, an exploration of the reckless glamour of the age and a feisty protagonist who you would love to have as your best friend.

To find out more and for news of new releases and giveaways, go to:

http://www.lbhathaway.com

Connect with L.B. Hathaway online:

(e) author@lbhathaway.com

(t) @LbHathaway

(f) https://www.facebook.com/pages/L-B-Hathaway-books/1423516601228019

(Goodreads) http://www.goodreads.com/author/show/8339051.L_B_Hathaway

Printed in Great Britain
by Amazon

18950591R00089